TORI MITCHELL

Second Chances in Sunset Cove

Sixth Street Books

Copyright © 2024 by Tori Mitchell

All rights reserved.

No part of this publication may be reproduced, distributed, or transmitted in any form or by any means, including photocopying, recording, or other electronic or mechanical methods, without the prior written permission of the publisher, except as permitted by U.S. copyright law.

This is a work of fiction. All characters, places, and events are products of the author's imagination or used in a fictitious manner. Any resemblance to actual persons (living or deceased) is coincidental.

Books written by Tori Mitchell

The Sunset Cove Series
Coming Home to Sunset Cove
Second Chances in Sunset Cove
Hometown Hero in Sunset Cove
Christmas in Sunset Cove
Finding Home in Sunset Cove

Sunset Cove Shorts
(July 2025 novellas)
The Christmas Inheritance
The Christmas Gift
The Christmas Surprise

Chapter One

Brook

WHEN BROOK REED GETS angry, she makes bread.

As the owner of Seaside Cupcakes in Sunset Cove, Brook set her own hours. She'd been at the bakery since four o'clock, taking out her frustration on baked goods. That's where Avery Brown, her best friend and employee, found her when she arrived for the morning shift.

Brook punched the dough into submission, letting out her frustration as she described last night's date. "Men are stupid," she muttered, slamming her hand into the dough again. "I don't know why I bother."

Avery slid the bowl of dough out of her reach. "That's enough kneading. You'll make the bread tough. Besides, your night couldn't have been all bad. Your last date went so well."

Brook sighed and walked over to the sink to wash her hands. She watched the bits of flour and soap rinse away, and tried to imagine her annoyance swirling down the drain as well. She dried her hands off and threw the towel onto a drying rack. "He had a motive. He needed a babysitter and tried to leave his son with me. I'm fine with kids. Just don't treat me like the built-in babysitter after one date."

Avery shook her head and grabbed the marker as she walked over to the baking board. She checked off bread, noting that Brook had made enough dough for ten extra loaves that morning.

Brook nodded at Avery and debated what to make next. Baking bread was her favorite task when she was mad, but even the more delicate desserts, like cupcakes and cookies, were a good distraction from her dating life. "Let's make some Sunset Cupcakes next. Those are popular with the tourists. Three dozen should do it, don't you think?"

Avery shrugged her shoulders. "You're the boss. Besides, this is my first winter at the bakery. It's been slow. Are you expecting a crowd this weekend?"

"It's almost Valentine's Day," Brook explained. "Love is in the air, and tourists are on their way. Speaking of love, Grant should be here soon. He wants to take measurements."

Avery frowned as she pulled trays of cupcake holders from the cabinet. "Are you sure? We're going to the courthouse after my shift is over. We're getting our marriage license today."

Avery and Grant had been engaged since Thanksgiving. Brook sighed as she considered her friends' whirlwind romance. They'd moved from dating to engaged in a short time, but their fast-moving relationship was built on a solid foundation. They'd been best friends for years.

Brook wasn't so lucky. She'd been on a few dates as a teenager, and one night out (with Avery's brother) that had plenty of sparks. But dating Brad Brown in her senior year of high school had turned out to be a bad idea.

She'd never told Avery about her date with Brad. Sparks or not, Brad didn't commit—and Brook was ashamed to think things would be different between them. That night had launched a decade of bad luck with men.

Brook drummed her fingers on the counter and checked her calendar. Time to focus on today, not the past. Grant was excited about the wedding, but it wasn't like him to overbook himself. She shrugged and pulled ingredients out to start the cupcakes. "He wants to measure the space and draw out some ideas. Maybe he thought it wouldn't take long. Grant thinks the place has a lot of potential."

"Of course it does," Avery agreed. "It was designed as a catering business, though. We have enough room to cook and bake, but there's not enough seating. You changed the subject too quickly, though. Did your date really want you to babysit?"

"It seemed that way. He introduced me to his little boy, handed me a diaper bag, and said he'd be back in an hour or two."

Avery's jaw dropped. "Did you let him leave?"

"Of course not. I handed back the diaper bag and said I'd be happy to have the kid join us on a date. I wasn't there to watch his kid while he did other things."

Avery shook her head again. "Good for you. I'd never dump my daughter on a stranger. Besides, I hope a stranger wouldn't just take Sophia. The world is a scary place."

Brook rolled her eyes and started measuring out flour. "The dating world is just as scary. It might be time to embrace being single. I'm almost thirty. Men want to date a younger woman who'll do whatever you ask. I've been told I'm too independent." She smirked. "They're probably right. I do like being independent."

Avery rested her head on Brook's shoulder. "Of course you're independent. Look at what you've done! You created a business from the ground up. You're an incredible woman."

She gave Brook's shoulder a squeeze, then gently took the measuring cup out of Brook's hand and spun her until they were face to face. "I'm an independent woman, too. I can raise Sophia and pay my own bills. But it's okay to want a partner in life. When I wanted to stay single, it just meant I hadn't found the right guy. Now that I've found Grant, we're partners in everything."

Brook shrugged as Avery's words hit her. She didn't want to be single forever, but Avery had found a good man. Not everyone was so lucky. "I've got a partner at the bakery. You're my partner! Unless you plan to quit once you get married." Her shoulders slumped as she considered the possibility. "You're not planning to quit, are you?"

"Of course not. I'm taking time off after the wedding, but I'll be back. I'm just saying that it's okay to look for someone, other than friends, to share your life with."

Brook grabbed the measuring cup and finished counting out cups of flour. "You're biased. Look at you, happily engaged to your best friend. I don't need a man to be happy."

Avery leaned against the counter and crossed her arms. "You're right. But you wouldn't go on dates if you wanted to stay single." She pushed away from the counter and started filling the cupcake trays with wrappers. "Besides, you know my ex-husband was a jerk. If it weren't for our daughter, I'd wish my first marriage had never happened. But everything happens for a reason. You've got to push through these bad dates to find the right guy."

Dating seemed pointless to Brook at this point. She hadn't grown up around functional, loving relationships. Her parents had separated after she graduated high school. Now they both lived in other cities, far away from Sunset Cove.

Brook's mother claimed they'd stayed married to give Brook a more stable childhood. It hadn't worked, though. In reality, her parents' marriage had failed long before it ended. All Brook had gotten from the experience was a skewed view of love. As a little girl, she'd thought marriage meant lies, arguments, and sleeping in different rooms.

As an adult, she knew better. But memories of her parents' marriage were burned clearly in her mind, reminding her of what could happen if a marriage went sour. For better or for worse, you were stuck with each other—until one person gave up and walked away.

She knew Avery was happy. She'd reconnected with Grant after moving back to Sunset Cove last year. They'd danced around each other for weeks, unwilling to date until Avery finalized her divorce. Now they were engaged.

Brook felt a thrill as she thought about the upcoming wedding. She was the maid of honor. And as much as Brook struggled to find love for herself, she loved weddings. She was thrilled to support both of her friends as they officially became husband and wife.

Not that she wanted a wedding of her own, of course. She was happy to be a bridesmaid instead of the bride.

Chapter Two

Brad

Brad Brown stood in the office of Grant Construction, watching the sun rise over Main Street. Sunset Cove, New Jersey hadn't changed much in the years he'd been gone. Their grandfather had raised Brad and Avery here, but both siblings had wandered far from their childhood home.

Brad had landed in Pittsburgh after college, following a friend who promised a job at his uncle's construction business.

The pay had been decent—when there was work. Brad's boss pushed employees to work endless hours over the spring and summer, only to lay them off each fall. Summer overtime didn't make up for the months without a paycheck. He'd worked odd jobs each winter to make ends meet.

When Avery invited Brad to visit Sunset Cove last Thanksgiving, he'd planned to stay for the weekend. She'd talked him into staying for the entire winter. It was nice spending time with his sister. They hadn't lived near each other in years. His niece, Sophia, was pretty cool, too.

Now Avery was marrying Grant Danielson, the owner of Grant Construction. She deserved a great guy in her life. Sophia did, too.

He'd lived in his sister's home for two months now, and worked with Avery's fiancé nearly as long. The timing had worked out. Grant wanted more time at home and needed to hire more employees. And here was Brad, a family member with years of construction experience.

Back in Pittsburgh, Brad had a reputation for being a serial dater. He got bored quickly, moving on to a new woman, a new adventure, every few weeks. He was ready to leave that behind. If his sister and Grant could have a fresh start, so could he.

Only one woman had caught his attention for any length of time. He'd blown it, though. He'd waited years to take Brook Reed on one date, kissed her until they were both senseless, then went back to his college campus without a word. No visits, no calls, no texts. He'd been a real jerk and too immature to realize that he was running from his feelings. While Brad wasn't proud of his actions, he didn't know how to fix things. So he'd just stayed away.

It had been easy enough to avoid Brook when he visited his grandfather in Sunset Cove. He'd stayed away from their favorite places and stuck close to home. When Brook opened her new bakery, he'd resisted the temptation to visit. He'd avoided the bakery and his former fling for years.

His luck was about to run out. They would both be in Avery and Grant's wedding party.

"Earth to Brad," Grant said, waving his hand in front of Brad's face. "Where'd you drift off?"

"Sorry, just daydreaming. What were we talking about?"

Grant picked up a pile of papers and handed them to Brad. "We're starting the plans for Brook's expansion today. Big changes for Seaside Cupcakes. She needs more seating in the dining area and outside. Encourage summer tourists to linger. It's almost February, so she's got one more rush of tourists coming. Now would be an ideal time to draw up plans. We can start renovations after Valentine's Day."

Brad looked warily at the papers in his hands. It was a standard contract for a business renovation, but the details were blank.

There were sheets for measurements, drawings, and estimated cost, all waiting to be filled out. "Sounds like a plan, boss. Are you headed there today to take measurements?"

Grant shook his head. "I'm applying for our marriage license today. Then we're meeting a local caterer to plan the reception."

Nick Butler, one of the first employees Grant had hired when he started the business, perked up at the mention of food. "Bring us some of those little finger sandwiches," he said, picking up a second stack of paper and leafing through the pages. "We'll help you finish the leftovers."

Grant just shook his head. "Doesn't your wife feed you? Brad, I'd like you to take the lead on this project. The goal is to expand Grant Construction. I need a second foreman. If you can handle this project from start to finish, I'd like to promote you."

"Hey, that's not fair. Brad will get all the free cupcakes," Nick objected. "Let me take this project."

Brad shifted his feet, surprised at the way Grant trusted him. He hadn't expected Grant to promote him so quickly, even if they were about to be brothers-in-law. He wasn't willing to fight Nick for the job.

Grant noticed his hesitation and turned to face both workers. "Nick, stop teasing Brad. He's taking point on this project."

His boss's confidence surprised Brad. A voice in his head said that this project might not be as simple as he hoped. It would take weeks to get the job done. Things might get awkward between him and Brook.

Hopefully, they wouldn't spend too much time together. She'd have to close the bakery while they were remodeling, wouldn't she? He perked up at that thought. Today could be the one day they worked together—while the bakery was still open. "What's our timeline? How long will the bakery be closed, and what's the reopening plan?"

Grant shook his head and glanced down at his desk calendar. Writing covered the giant grid. Brad couldn't make sense of it, but Grant treated it like an ironclad schedule that guided their daily jobs. "Brook's not closing. She'll need to stop using the kitchen while we do demolition, but her plan is to work around us. She's already stockpiling cupcakes and cookies."

Brad raised his eyebrows. He knew Brook was stubborn, but didn't realize she would attempt to run her bakery without a working kitchen. "It's her decision, I guess. How does that change the deadline?"

"It's your project. Finalize the renovation plans, and get the job done without interrupting her workflow too much. I think you're up for the challenge."

Brad looked at Nick, who had tucked his own paperwork into a clipboard and tugged on his coat. Brad grabbed his own clipboard and stuffed the papers inside. "Let's get started, then. When do we leave?"

Nick held up his clipboard and shrugged. "I was messing with you. You're on your own today. I'm meeting with the hospital about a new children's ward. The project's bigger than anything we've done before, but they're on a tight deadline and hiring a few companies to get the job done faster."

Brad gulped. His last boss had kept Brad as a low-ranking crew member, but Grant wanted his workers to take on more responsibility. Apparently, that meant he'd be spending a lot of time alone at the bakery.

As much as Brad wanted to step away from this project, he needed to patch up his rift with Brook—for everyone's sake. He'd avoided Brook for far too long.

Nick noticed his discomfort and put out a hand to stop Brad from picking up his coat. "What's wrong? Don't want to work with your sister?"

Brad gave a dry chuckle and tried to sidestep Nick. "It's not a problem. I can handle this project."

But Nick wouldn't let it go. He continued to stare at his friend, then cocked his head. "What is it, then? Got a crush on Brook?"

Brad gave an impatient huff and zipped up his jacket, then reached for his tool belt and paperwork. "Don't worry about it. I'll be back. I've got to measure a few things and work on these plans."

He climbed into his truck and leaned back in the seat. It looked like he would be spending a lot more time with Brook Reed.

Chapter Three

Brook

AFTER SLIDING A BATCH of Sunset Cupcakes into the oven, Brook practically pushed Avery out the door. She wanted her friend to have time to clean up and get to the courthouse. They'd reschedule her kitchen measurements later.

Now that she had a few minutes alone, Brook studied her plans for the wedding cake. After letting the couple pick out the theme and flavors, they'd asked Brook to surprise them with the design. This cake was her gift to the happy couple. Brook hoped they would like it.

Determined to remain in a good mood, Brook shoved aside any lingering thoughts about last night's date. She'd already blocked the guy's number on her phone. She'd learned a long time ago to pay attention to a man's actions, rather than his words.

Brook liked to keep things simple. She didn't let people take advantage of her, and she wasn't one to give men a second chance.

She tucked away her notebook, satisfied with her design for the cake. Brook hummed to herself as she restocked their display case for the afternoon. The display was a relic from the previous owner, her old catering boss. It was small and older, but Brook made it work. It added a touch of nostalgia to the shop. They should include the case when they renovated.

The floor plan and color scheme needed updating, though. Something bright and beachy. The bakery's dark-stained wooden walls were professional, which suited a catering business, but a bakery by the ocean should be cheerful and inviting.

"Sky blue would work," she said out loud, talking to herself as she walked around the empty bakery. Brook stopped to examine the colorful cupcake painted on her largest wall. "If we're painting the walls, we should redesign the logo, too. Maybe an orange sunset to complement the blue."

Brook loved this time of day. The morning rush was over, and people looking for after-lunch treats wouldn't be here for another hour. Brook grabbed a fresh notepad and sketched out ideas for a new logo, then went back into the kitchen. It was time to bake pies. Warm apple pie with a scoop of ice cream always sold well after lunch.

She gathered flour, sugar and the butter she'd left out to soften. Start with the pie crusts, then add the filling she'd mixed this morning.

It was quiet without Avery. That was okay, though. She was going to enjoy the peacefulness. She'd only hired Avery as her first employee a few months ago. It wasn't like she needed company.

But just as she settled into the routine of sifting and measuring, the kitchen's back door flew open. Brook shrieked in surprise. The measuring cup in her hand flew into the air, scattering flour everywhere—even on the man who had opened the door.

Her eyes narrowed as Avery's brother stepped into the room. "What are you doing here? That door was locked."

Brad held his hands up in surrender, a key hanging from his finger. "Grant gave me the key. He thought you'd be busy out front, since you're working alone."

"Grant gave you a key to my bakery. Why would he do that?"

Brad pulled a clipboard out from under his arm, holding it out to her. "I work at Grant Construction now, remember? Grant put me in charge of the bakery's renovations."

Brook closed her eyes and began counting to ten. That's what her school guidance counselor had told her to do when she was upset at school. If she closed her eyes long enough, Brad might go away.

Or maybe she was hallucinating. The memories of her first awful date—her night out with Brad, the one that had started her unlucky streak—were coming back to haunt her. She counted to twelve for good measure, then let out a long breath and opened her eyes.

No luck. Brad still stood in her kitchen, covered in a light dusting of flour.

He watched her with raised eyebrows. "Are you okay? You're not having a seizure or something, are you? I can go get help."

Brook snorted. If she hadn't known Brad was working with Grant, she'd think for sure this was a hallucination. Brad didn't offer to get help for people.

Brad would stomp your heart and leave you bleeding on the floor.

Maybe that was too harsh. After all, he was her best friend's brother. They'd both be in Avery's wedding, too. She needed to be civil with him. Brook bit her tongue, grabbed a towel, and tossed it in Brad's direction. "Sorry about the flour. You surprised me. I wasn't expecting anyone today."

He nodded and caught the towel, then stepped back through the doorway and brushed his jacket off outside. His thoughtfulness surprised Brook. Most people would dust off where they stood. There was already flour on the floor. While he finished up, she began sweeping.

A few moments later, a pair of large, callused hands tugged the broom away from her. Brad grinned. "Let me clean up. It's my fault. The least I can do is sweep."

Brook stood back and watched as he swept the flour into a neat pile, then used a dustpan to scoop it into the trash. She would not admire the view while he cleaned the floor. No, she would not. She turned her back to him, busying herself in the refrigerator while she tried to get the image of his snug jeans out of her head. She pulled out the pie filling and whirled around, bumping into Brad as she did so.

Brad reached out a hand to steady her, grabbing the bowl with his other hand. "Take it easy. I don't think apples will clean up as easily as flour."

Brook bristled at his touch, annoyed to feel a spark where his hand touched bare skin. What was up with that? She yanked the bowl from his hand. "Thanks, but I've got it. Why are you here today? Grant didn't mention assigning someone else to the project."

He shrugged. "I was surprised, too. Grant's got his hands full with the wedding, and he's trying to expand the business. He needs a second foreman." He attempted to grin, but the smile didn't light up his face the way it usually did. "I'm at your service and ready to design your bakery renovations."

Brook held back a groan. Grant was one of her best friends, and she'd been looking forward to working with him. Now she'd need to work with Brad instead. Brook hadn't seen Brad in almost a decade—not since their one and only date. He'd clearly been avoiding her for years, and she was okay with that.

If he was in charge of the bakery renovations, they couldn't avoid each other.

But if she understood one thing, it was the need to delegate. Grant had been stretched thin for years. He worked nearly every weekend, getting jobs done and filling in the gaps as his business grew beyond the ability of his small crew. Even though she wasn't happy about working with Brad, she was glad Grant had shared some of his workload.

For that reason, and that reason alone, she would remain professional with Brad. She attempted to smile back at him while she set the pie filling on the counter. "In that case, let's get started. What do you need from me today?"

"We need to talk about your design plans. Do you want to talk now, or should I start measuring while you finish your work?"

Surprised by his thoughtfulness, Brook gestured toward her work in progress. "Start measuring. Let me finish these pies and get them in the oven. It won't take long. Then I'll catch up with you."

He nodded and pulled out a tape measure, writing down basic dimensions while she cut the butter into her pie crust. She watched him out of the corner of her eye. He seemed competent enough, confidently measuring the kitchen area before moving to the customer's side.

She shook her head. While she knew Brad was back in town, she'd never thought he would work in her bakery. He was part of her past—a part of her life that hadn't seen daylight in years. Now she'd see him every day. Wasn't life strange?

She filled the pie crusts, quickly weaved together the lattice toppings, and slid the finished pies into the oven. Then she set a timer and washed her hands. It was time to play nice with Brad. Brook didn't give guys second chances, but letting him renovate the bakery didn't mean she had to date him. They just had to see each other every day. Nothing awkward about that.

Brook rolled her eyes before she pushed through the swinging door and out of the kitchen. While she'd expected Brad to be measuring things and taking notes, he was standing next to the cash register, looking at a newspaper clipping.

She cleared her throat to get his attention. "Clint Brown was my very first customer. The newspaper took his picture at my grand opening. He loved my double-chocolate muffins."

Brad jumped, his face flushing as he turned to face her. "I didn't realize my grandpa was here so often. He didn't mention it. I wish he had. I could have come here with him."

"Would you? I thought you were avoiding me."

Brad's blush deepened. He sighed. "Look, I'm sorry about the way I treated you. I shouldn't have avoided you for so long. We can talk about your design plans now, if you've got time. Or I can ask Grant to assign someone else to the job. It's your choice."

Guilt rushed through Brook. Not because of what she'd said to Brad about avoiding her. He'd deserved that comment. But she wouldn't make more work for Grant. She'd just have to deal with Brad for as long as it took to remodel the bakery.

She waved off his concerns and pasted on another fake smile. "It was one kiss, ten years ago. I've practically forgotten about it."

"Ouch. That hurt. You still don't pull your punches."

His reply made Brook burst out with a genuine laugh. "Okay, I haven't forgotten about it. But we were kids, and we're going to put it behind us. We were friends once. We can be friendly again."

Brad nodded and held out his hand. "Let's shake on it. We'll put the past behind us and have a second chance at friendship."

Brook took his hand and shook it, then yanked her hand back. She'd felt sparks again when they touched. This was ridiculous. No one felt sparks in real life. She cleared her throat and gestured toward his clipboard. "Should we get started?"

They started in the kitchen, discussing the existing setup and what Brook wanted to change. She needed more oven space and cooling racks, and fewer stovetops.

"We could rip out one traditional oven and stack a double oven in its place," Brad offered. "The two gas stovetops are wasted space."

Brook agreed on the ovens.

They didn't agree with the changes at the front of the store. "This display case needs to go," Brad said, resting a hand on the oversized case.

Brook's jaw fell at his suggestion. "It's an antique! It's been in this store for decades."

"It's beautiful, but it's too bulky. A streamlined case would give you room for two additional tables here. You'll also have more room to store your pies and cakes. Grant says you spend a lot of time moving products from the kitchen to the storefront. This would save you steps and let you show more variety at one time."

But Brook put her foot down. She wouldn't let Brad boss her around and take over the project. This was her bakery, after all. Not his. "The display case stays."

He shrugged. "Consider it. You need more table space, and the display takes up a lot of room. Sometimes the easiest solution is best."

Brook choked back a laugh. Brad did know how to take the easy way out. That didn't make it the right choice.

Chapter Four

Brad

Brad couldn't keep his mind off Brook. She seemed to follow him home, intruding on his every thought on the short drive through town.

He thought of her at the grocery store, where he would "accidentally" run into her and her friends after class. He thought about her as they passed the movie theater, where they'd had their one and only date. She even snuck into his thoughts as he pulled up to his grandfather's old house. Brook had done most of her high school baking experiments in the Brown kitchen.

He shook off the ghosts of his past and focused on what needed to be done. His sister and Grant weren't home yet, so it was a great time to finish up the paperwork on Brook's bakery and review his notes.

One perk of living with the boss, he thought. He knows I'm working, even when I'm not in the office.

Brad settled down at the kitchen table and pulled out his drawings and dimensions. That antique display case added character, but it also took up a ton of space. He'd try to talk her out of keeping it. His job was to make the bakery look its best—not to drag relics into a new project.

He had to admire Brook's tenacity, though. She was as feisty as he remembered. It wouldn't surprise him if she ended up keeping the old display case. It was her bakery, after all. She'd have a final say in all the plans.

He admired a woman who knew what she wanted and spoke her mind.

He looked over his notes and added to them, being sure to include Brook's comments and his own thoughts. It was tough to stay focused when all he could think about was the kiss he'd shared with Brook.

Brad hadn't been in a serious relationship since... ever. There was just something about Brook that made him want to jump in feet-first.

Just like high school, she'd smelled like vanilla and honeysuckle today. She smelled like she'd baked all day, then took a walk through a wildflower field. He shook his head, trying to clear his thoughts. Brad had no right to be attracted to her. He'd had a chance with her, and he'd blown it. This whole mess was his fault.

The front door slammed, interrupting his thoughts. Two pairs of feet ambled through the house before joining him in the kitchen.

Avery held up a white envelope with the Sunset Cove registrar's logo. "We got the marriage license! One more step closer to the wedding."

Grant held out a white box that smelled of fresh-baked bread. "I got the little sandwich samples, too. Don't tell Nick, because I'm not sharing." He grinned and opened the box, pulling out a tiny sandwich and finishing it in one bite. "How did it go at Brook's bakery?"

Brad would never admit to his sister or boss that Brook was driving him crazy. Something about that girl made his brain go haywire. Grant might understand, but it didn't seem right to talk about Brook like that in front of her friends. "It went fine," he said instead. "I got the dimensions, and we talked about the floor plan."

Grant nodded and pulled out a chair. He examined the paperwork in front of them. "She wants to keep the old display case. Talk her out of it, will you? It breaks up the flow and doesn't fit her needs as she expands the bakery."

"She seems set on keeping the display." Brad shrugged. "It's up to her, isn't it? I don't want to push her."

Grant threw his head back and laughed. "Brook doesn't let people push her around. Show her the benefits of a new display case. If she won't let the old one go, we'll work around it. It might mean fewer seats for customers, though. Remind her of that."

He stood up and walked out of the kitchen, humming to himself as he tugged another sandwich out of the box. Brad looked at his sister and shrugged. "I don't think you're getting any of those sandwiches. How did the wedding plans go?"

"Today went well. Want some coffee?" After he nodded, Avery walked to the cabinet and pulled out two cups, then started the coffeemaker. A grin stretched across her face. "Everything's coming together."

"Glad to hear that. Is there anything I can do?"

Avery bit her lip, watching the coffee drip into the pot. "Now that you mention it..." Her smile grew impossibly wide as she poured two cups of coffee, then joined Brad at the table. "I know you're already in the wedding, but I have a favor to ask."

Brad grabbed the mug of black coffee and took a sip. "What do you need? You know I'm willing to help."

"I don't need help, exactly. Just your support. I'd like you to be a bridesman."

Brad set the mug of coffee back on the table, his brow creased with confusion. "What's that?"

"A bridesman stands on the bride's side. I know it's traditional for the men to support the groom, but I've only got one brother. Now that Grandpa is gone, you and Sophia are my only family."

Brad stared at the table as he considered Avery's request. "You've got Grant. He's part of your family now. Besides, I haven't been a great brother or uncle. When I moved back to Sunset Cove, Sophia barely knew who I was."

Avery reached out to grab his hand. "That's my fault," she mumbled. "I let my ex-husband boss me around, and keep me away from my family. It's got nothing to do with you." She sat up taller and smiled, her eyes filling with tears. "Besides, who was the first person I called when I got to Sunset Cove? I called you. And when I thought we'd lose this house to the tax office? We talked every day."

Brad cleared his throat. "Grant did most of the work, and Brook gave you a job. I didn't do much."

Avery reached out and gave him a friendly smack on the shoulder. "You don't give yourself enough credit. You called every day, trying to fix our problems. And now you're living here, and we're making up for lost time. My daughter loves you. I love you. We both want you to stand on our side for the wedding."

Brad chuckled and shook his head. "I'd do anything for you. You don't need to bring the kid into it. But if it means that much to you and Sophia, I'll do it. I'll be your bridesman, or whatever you called it."

Avery jumped out of the chair and threw her arms around Brad. "I'm so excited! Wait until I tell Brook."

Brad froze in his chair, too surprised to move. "What does Brook have to do with it?"

"She's my maid of honor, silly. You'll stand next to her during the wedding." Avery let out a happy sigh. "Sophia already calls her Aunt Brook, so it will be like her aunt and uncle are both there with us. We'll be surrounded by so much love."

Brad held back a groan. He'd known Brook was in the wedding, of course. He just hadn't visualized where a bridesman might stand. But if it meant this much to Avery, he'd do it. He was already working alongside Brook at the bakery. He could get through this, too.

Still, he didn't want to make things awkward. He keep his hands, and his eyes, to himself. No more daydreaming about Brook. No flirting. And he definitely couldn't think about the kiss they'd shared while she was in high school.

Before that date, chasing girls had been fun. Brook was different. He wanted something more, some deeper connection. Part of him still wanted that with Brook, even though it was obvious she didn't feel the same.

Brad began to sweat as he realized how much time he would spend with Brook. Could he do this? He wasn't sure, and cautiously asked Avery one last time if being a bridesman was a good idea. "What does Grant think about this? Doesn't he think it's weird that I'll be standing with the ladies?"

She waved off his concern and laughed. "He's used to my weirdness. He's okay with it."

"If Grant's okay with it, I guess I am, too."

Brad pasted a smile on his face, and tried not to imagine how awkward the next few weeks could be.

Chapter Five

Brook

The bell above Seaside Cupcake's door jingled cheerfully, and Brook hustled out of the kitchen to greet her customer. She stopped short when she saw Grant standing in front of the cash register.

Grant offered her a grin. "I'd like a dozen double-chocolate muffins, please. The crew will be mad if I don't get them anything."

Brook cocked her head. They had been friends for years, but he rarely stopped by on a weekday morning. Grant was knee-deep in renovations by this time of day. "Is that all you're here for? Just muffins?"

"I might be here for something else, but let's get the muffins first."

She nodded, then grabbed a box and filled it with Grant's order. Double-chocolate muffins had always been Grant's favorite. They were popular with the tourists, too. "Avery just left on her break," she said, continuing to box up the treats. "She's taking Sophia to school. But you know that. She should be back in thirty minutes."

Grant nodded. "I was hoping to catch you alone. Hope that's okay."

"You're always welcome here. What do you need?"

Grant drummed his hands on the countertop and seemed to consider his words. "We need to talk about Brad."

Brook hesitated as she reached for the last muffin. Of all the topics he could bring up, she hadn't expected this. "Okay, let's talk about him. Is he a convicted felon? Does he have a secret family of twelve children back in Pittsburgh? He doesn't seem the type to have a secret family, but it's been a long time since I've known him."

Grant barked out a laugh. "It's nothing like that. I thought I'd be remodeling your bakery, but there's not enough time." He paused and ran his hands through his hair, looking guilty. "We can meet your deadline if Brad does the work. If I take charge of this project myself, there's no way you'll get done before summer. But I want you to be okay with this. I should have talked to you before sending him over."

Brook looked up, surprise flooding her face. "Of course I'm okay with this. I know what it's like to be overwhelmed. You need time to focus on your new wife and daughter, too." She paused, taking a deep breath as she thought of her own schedule. "I get it. And I'm happy for you."

Grant raised his eyebrows. "Are you sure?"

"Yes, I'm sure. It's fine. We can all work together."

Grant leaned against the counter and considered his friend for a moment. "You guys never dated or anything, did you?"

Brook laughed nervously. She carefully arranged her face in a neutral expression, knowing that it was pointless. Grant was one of her best friends. He knew all of her tells. "Why would you say that?"

"Just a hunch. You blush every time I mention his name. And Brad changes the subject when I talk about you."

Brook felt her face heat up. How embarrassing! She needed to work harder at hiding her thoughts about Brad. They were just friends, and it needed to stay that way.

Grant laughed at her expression. "I'm teasing you. As long as you're comfortable with Brad working in the bakery, I'm confident that he'll do a great job. I saw his sketches last night. You're in good hands."

Brook couldn't help herself. She blushed again as she thought about Brad's hands in her hair, playing down her spine. Just the thought gave her shivers.

Now is not the time, she thought. She cleared her throat and smiled at Grant. "I totally understand. Sophia needs a dad right now. She needs stability. Avery should be able to spend time with her new husband, too. I know you'll be watching over the project, even if you and Nick aren't in charge. I trust everyone on your crew."

Grant let out a sigh of relief. "I appreciate it. I've been so busy that my head is spinning. If I can train Brad as our second foreman and split the crew for our smaller projects, it will take some pressure off me."

The two friends chatted briefly before Grant paid for his muffins and left. The bell gave another cheerful jingle as he exited, leaving Brook alone in the bakery.

She wouldn't be alone for long, of course. Avery would be back in a few minutes. Still, she wondered what it was like to have enough employees to take time off for herself. Avery was a big help, but between her daughter and other commitments, there was no way her friend could take over the bakery for a few days.

Brook enjoyed being in charge. It was one reason she'd started her own business. But wouldn't it be nice if she could hand over the reins sometimes? If she could step back and take a short break.

She let out a laugh. It would be wonderful to have time off. That would never happen—and besides, what would she do with herself if she didn't have work? Brook had committed herself to the bakery. She barely had a life outside these walls. If she wanted to get together with her friends, she invited them here for treats. By the time her day was done, she had almost no time or energy left.

On that note, it was time for caffeine. Brook normally stuck to black coffee, but she deserved a treat today. She started to prepare a sweet, creamy latte for herself.

Brook was pouring the final touches of frothed milk into her cup when the store bell rang again. She held back a sigh as three older ladies bustled into the shop. Maybe her latte would stay warm long enough for her to enjoy it. She couldn't let the tourists know that she'd hoped for a break. Brook smiled and greeted them, asking how she could help them.

The shortest of the three spoke first. "I want a slice of apple pie." She turned to her friends and nodded knowingly. "Apples are a fruit, so apple pie is fine for breakfast."

Brook held back a smile. She wasn't the first customer to make that argument. Unfortunately, Brook wouldn't bake today's pies until closer to lunchtime. "I'm sorry, the apple pie won't be ready until noon. I have some apple cinnamon rolls this morning. They're close to pie, except for the caramel glaze."

The woman crossed her arms. "No pie. What kind of bakery is this?" she huffed. "Give me a double-chocolate muffin instead."

But Brook had just sold the last of the double-chocolate muffins to Grant. Hadn't she erased it from the board? She turned around, confirming that the muffins were still listed. She sighed, sensing that this customer wouldn't be happy with substitutes. Still, she needed to try. It was important to keep her customers happy. "I ran out of those muffins a few minutes ago. If you're interested in chocolate treats, I have peanut butter-chocolate muffins, cocoa cookies, and some chocolate cupcakes."

"Peanut butter? I'm allergic to peanuts!" the customer shrieked. "Are you trying to kill me?"

Brook took a step back, holding up her hands. "I'm sorry. I didn't know. We're careful to avoid cross-contamination in the kitchen. I'm happy to get you some fresh cookies or cupcakes that haven't been in the display case with the peanut butter muffins."

But the woman shook her head sharply. "Edith, Sharon, get what you want. I'm clearly not welcome here. Offering me peanuts," she muttered. "Ridiculous."

Brook was losing her patience, but kept her smile in place for the next customer. "How can I help you?"

Edith stepped forward and pointed to the cocoa cookies. "Can I have a half-dozen cookies? How much will that be?"

Brook gestured toward the menu board, where the prices were listed. "It's eight dollars for six cookies, or fourteen dollars for a dozen."

"No, no. That's far too expensive. I can make dozens of cookies at home for that price."

Brook closed her eyes for a moment. Yes, she was definitely losing her patience. "My prices are comparable to every bakery in the nearby towns. The cost of ingredients has gone up, so I've had to increase my prices as well."

The woman named Sharon stepped forward and waved Edith away from the counter. "I'll pay for the cookies. Now, what about that pie? Maybe if we waited a few minutes?"

"She said the pies wouldn't be ready until lunchtime. Unless you think she's just refusing to sell them to us," the first lady piped up. "I wouldn't put it past her."

The door over the bakery rang again, and Brook glanced up with dread. She needed to deal with these women before she took on any other customers.

The person walking in wasn't a customer, though. Brad Brown stood in the doorway, cautiously eyeing the squabbling women before he stepped into the bakery and let the door swing shut behind him.

Edith raised her eyebrows and paused her arguing to admire the newcomer. "Hi, handsome. I hope you don't want pie. And I hope you're not allergic to peanut butter. You might want to leave. We're going across the bridge to Sea City instead. I've heard they have a great bakery."

Brad's jaw dropped at the woman's boldness. Despite her annoyance, Brook held back a giggle. This wasn't her first pair of difficult tourists, and it wouldn't be the last. The best way to deal with these types of customers was to be firm but friendly. She hoped he wouldn't start arguing with them.

But Brad didn't fight back or argue with the women. Instead, he walked over to the display case. "I'll never pass up an apple cinnamon roll with the caramel glaze. They're my favorite. And a small black coffee, please?"

Brook busied herself behind the counter with his order. When she was done, Brad handed Brook a twenty-dollar bill and winked. "Keep the change. These cinnamon rolls are worth it."

He whistled as he walked out the door, clutching his treat and coffee. But instead of climbing into the truck parked out front, he strolled past his vehicle and into the side alley that led to her back door. He was going into the bakery's kitchen!

Brook heard the back door unlock and open as the women began gabbing again.

"I want what the handsome young man ordered," Edith said, running a hand through her hair. "One apple cinnamon roll and a black coffee, please. Sharon, Sally, what do you say? I never liked fussy coffees. And those rolls look delicious."

Sally nodded. "They're not pie, but they'll do. Make it three rolls and three coffees. I want mine with extra cream and sugar."

Brook hid her smile as she packed up the baked goods in a takeout container (no need to tempt them to linger) and poured three coffees. The women haggled over who was paying before they finally settled their tab and left. Brook closed her eyes for a moment, hoping that the worst of the craziness was over, then walked back into the kitchen.

Brad sat at the kitchen island, licking caramel from his fingers. He grinned as she walked into the room. "Are they gone? Did they order anything?"

Brook slumped into the chair next to him and sighed. "They're gone. They were ready to leave without ordering, but got what the 'handsome young man' ordered instead. How did you do that?"

He tipped his head back and laughed. "I was measuring the old oven and heard them arguing. They were too busy complaining to realize that there were plenty of decent options. They just needed someone to push them in the right direction."

Brook shook her head in amazement, then stood up and walked toward the pantry. She'd need to replace the double-chocolate muffins that Grant had ordered. She'd start the pies once Avery returned, too. Then she stopped to look back at Brad. "I'm sorry, I should get your change. You were putting on a show. You didn't need to leave a tip."

Brad held up a hand to stop her. "I don't mind tipping. You've got a lot of expenses coming up." A hopeful look crossed his face. "But maybe, for such a generous tip, I could have a second cinnamon roll?"

Brook laughed again. Brad may have broken her heart in high school, but he'd always been able to make her laugh. It was nice to have him back in Sunset Cove, even if she still wasn't convinced that he was staying for long. She plucked two more cinnamon rolls out of the case and put them on a plate. By the time she'd returned,

Brad was sipping coffee and scrolling through an appliance website on his laptop.

He rubbed his hands together when he saw the full plate. "Excellent. Your cinnamon rolls are the best."

"You haven't been to my bakery since we opened. How did you know my cinnamon rolls were so good?"

"You made them a few times at Grandpa's house. I always grabbed extras to take back to my dorm room. I didn't share them with my roommate, either."

Brook remembered Brad's appetite. He'd been first in line when she baked in the Brown's kitchen. It was easier to use Avery's house, rather than listen to her own parents argue and hope she didn't get caught in the middle. The Brown family hadn't complained—they'd always enjoyed sampling her treats. If she remembered correctly, Brad rarely waited until the old kitchen timer went off to join her. He sat in the kitchen with a plate, waiting patiently.

She hadn't minded the company. It had been a little distracting to have her crush in the kitchen, though. She'd been shocked when he asked her out, but not all that surprised when he'd disappeared afterward. Brad wasn't known for his long-term commitments, even back in high school.

Their failed date had meant the end of keeping her company in the kitchen. That didn't mean they couldn't be friendly now, though. She pulled out a chair and gestured toward the laptop. "What are you looking at?"

"I'd like to order the new appliances for your kitchen. Depending on what you want, it could take time to get your order."

That made sense to Brook. Grant often complained that supply chain issues were slowing down his projects. Better to order what you need now, than risk waiting weeks past the deadline for a stove to arrive. She scrolled through the site, stopping at a double oven that seemed wider than usual. "Would this fit? We could prep for the town's festivals more quickly if we had a larger oven."

Brad nodded and jotted down the model number. "We can make almost anything fit. It's just a matter of working around the appliances."

She watched him work, sketching out floor plan ideas for two different oven sizes, and even giving her ideas of how they might keep her existing gas stove and oven to save time and money. Brook left the kitchen twice to help customers, returning each time to Brad's side.

The ladies in the bakery hadn't been wrong. He was handsome enough. He was easy to work with, too. It was a shame he'd been so thoughtless in high school. If she was going to give anyone a second chance at her heart, it might be Brad Brown.

Brook jerked back, nearly toppling her chair in the process. Where had that thought come from? She didn't give guys a second chance. If they broke your heart once, they shouldn't get to try again.

Brad glanced over in concern. "You okay?"

She stood up and nodded. "I'm fine. I've got to finish the morning's baking. Do you mind? I can check in with you once the muffins are in the oven. Your sister will be back in a few minutes, too. Then we won't be interrupted by customers."

He continued sketching and looking up appliance dimensions while she measured and mixed batter. It was peaceful, those few minutes while they worked on their separate projects. She could see herself settling down with someone like this. It would be nice to have a man who stopped by the bakery for a cup of coffee and some company. He'd quietly finish paperwork in the kitchen, spending time together, but not acting like her own work wasn't important.

It was hard to find a man who valued her job as much as their own. Brad had been patient, understanding that her baking and customers came first.

It was a shame she could never be more than friends with Brad.

Chapter Six

Brad

BRAD PATTED HIS FULL stomach as he walked out of Seaside Cupcakes. That third cinnamon roll had hit the spot.

He didn't regret standing up for Brook when those three ladies were bothering her. Why did women bully each other? He'd never understand it.

Brad enjoyed working on his drawings in Brook's bakery. The kitchen was warm and welcoming. The delicious smells and cinnamon rolls were a bonus. When his sister had gotten back from school drop-off, he'd gone over his ideas with Brook. They both agreed that the extra-wide double oven would be her best option. She'd lose counter space, but triple the amount of food she could bake at one time.

He spent the rest of the day driving around town, filing building permits at city hall and ordering a dumpster for the back of the bakery. They wouldn't need it until after the wedding, but it was better to line these things up ahead of time.

Avery was home when he stopped by for a late lunch. With the wedding date drawing near, Brad knew he'd need to find somewhere else to live soon. He didn't want to overstay his welcome or intrude on her growing family. Still, he was grateful for the time he'd spent catching up with his sister and niece.

Brad made himself a sandwich and grabbed a can of soda, then sat at the table with Avery. "How was work?"

"It was good," she said. "After you left, Brook couldn't stop talking about the plans you shared with her. She's excited about the new oven. And we'll need the extra seating in the spring." Avery clapped her hands with excitement. "I'm so proud of Brook. It's been fun watching her business grow. I even get to work with you, big brother. Who would have thought? All the pieces of my life are coming together."

Brad took a bite from his sandwich and shrugged. "Your fiance owns the construction business. Maybe he wanted me to spend time with you. I don't think Brook enjoys having me in charge, though."

"I'm getting weird vibes from Brook. Did something happen between the two of you?" Avery raised her eyebrows, giving Brad a look that likely made Sophia spill all her secrets.

He coughed and choked on the lettuce in his sandwich. Brad shook his head and took a deep drink. When he'd recovered, he asked, "Why would you say that?"

"I'm not sure. You act differently around her. Sometimes you dated and dumped girls fast enough that I didn't notice." Avery picked up her cup and swirled the coffee around. "I'm being ridiculous. Brook was my best friend. I know if she dated my brother."

Brad tugged at his sweatshirt collar. Was it hot in here? "We didn't... I mean, we didn't really date. Things got awkward between us, though."

She gave him a knowing look. "Awkward, huh?"

Brad took another drink as he considered his options. If his sister found out he'd walked out on Brook after one date, he was toast. She'd never let it go. "We're better now. We worked at the bakery while you were gone today. It was okay."

Avery closed her eyes for a moment and sighed. "You're my brother and I love you, but you will not hurt my friend. You have a habit of leaving broken hearts everywhere you go."

Brad set his soda down with a clink. "I'm not that bad."

"I didn't bother learning your girlfriends' names in high school! There were too many to remember."

"There were not!"

"Those girls remembered you, though," Avery continued. She rolled her eyes. "They wrote your name all over the bathroom stalls. I couldn't wait for you to graduate."

She grew serious as she leaned over the kitchen table, reaching out to touch Brad's hand. "Brook's been through a lot of bad dates. She doesn't need to add my brother to her list. I know she's attractive, but she's not just another woman. She's my best friend. Please don't hurt her."

Brad sat back in his chair, stunned. He hadn't realized his attraction to Brook was so obvious. Not that he intended to do anything about that attraction—his sister's best friend was off limits. He'd broken Brook's heart once already. Even if Avery didn't know their backstory, Brook didn't give second chances.

"Brook's a beautiful woman, but I've got no intention of dating her." *This time*, he thought. "Brook feels the same way. She made that clear when we started working together. We're just friends. Barely friends, in fact. Nothing more."

Even as he said those words, he remembered how his hands felt woven into Brook's hair while they kissed. She was cute, hard-working, and a fantastic kisser. He was ready to leave his heartbreaker reputation behind him, but suspected that any attempt to date Brook wouldn't end well. They should stay away from each other.

Avery's eyebrows rose as she stared her brother down. "Be sure. I just got Brook back as my best friend. Besides, you're in the wedding together. Don't make this awkward for all of us."

Brad nodded as he stood to clear both their plates off the table. "I'm sure. We've got a bakery to remodel, and a wedding to plan. We won't have time to *think* about dating."

She laughed and stood up from the table, then walked over to give her brother a hug. "You've never let a lack of time stop you from dating before, but you've matured since college. I'm glad you moved back to Sunset Cove." She stepped out of their embrace and checked the time on her phone. "I've got to start supper and take a shower before Sophia's bus gets here. You're welcome to eat with us, of course."

Brad watched Avery bustle around the kitchen as she spoke. She pulled a pot roast out of the fridge, then melted some butter in a large pan.

He leaned against the counter and crossed his arms. His sister worked hard at everything she did. She deserved a night off.

That gave him an idea. He didn't have the skills to cook a full meal, but he could help with the full-time mom gig. "Let me have Sophia for the night. We'll go for a walk and watch the sunset. Get some pizza. Give you and Grant time alone."

Avery turned her back to the stove, letting the meat brown as she considered his offer. "Are you turning down a pot roast? It's your favorite meal."

He gave his sister the same cocky grin he'd given dozens of women. It wouldn't make his sister swoon, of course, but it usually got him what he wanted. "Save some leftovers for me. Enjoy some quiet time before the wedding."

I'm sure you're ready to get me out of your hair, too, he thought. Brad already felt guilty that he was spending so much time with his sister's family. He'd looked into apartments around town, but couldn't afford any of them on a construction worker's salary. The rental homes in Sunset Cove were priced for tourists and short-term visitors, not permanent residents. Since he planned to stick around, he'd need to find a place he could afford after the wedding.

While he wasn't moving out tonight, he could give Avery and Grant one night alone. He knew Grant loved Sophia, but it had to be tough getting married to someone who already had a child. His sister and fiance deserved at least a little kid-free time.

Plus, he liked the squirt. He'd never realized how fun it was to be an uncle until he moved in with Avery and Sophia.

Brad was standing by his truck when Sophia's school bus rolled to the curb. He waved her forward and lifted her in an uncle-sized bear hug.

"Uncle Brad! Why are you home?" Sophia asked. Brad felt a flash of guilt. He and Grant worked long days, even during the winter—something he knew Grant was trying to change as they expanded the business.

He pushed down the guilt, then grinned and opened the truck door for his niece. "I'm home for you, kiddo. We're getting pizza and going for a walk on the beach. I brought blankets, hats, and hot cocoa. It'll be fun."

Sophia cheered and declared, "I love the beach. Even when it's cold outside, I'd rather be in the sand than inside the house."

"I agree, kid. The beach is a great place. It shouldn't get too cold while the sun's out."

Their first stop was the boardwalk's pizza shop, where Brad ordered a pizza with extra cheese and pepperoni. They watched the few tourists in town walk past the restaurant, enjoying the last hours of daylight on an unseasonably warm day.

Once their food was ready, he carried the pizza and blankets down the boardwalk and onto the sand. Sophia paced the beach for a few minutes, searching for the perfect place to eat dinner.

Brad stood back and watched with amusement. He'd done the same thing when he brought girls here on dates. You wanted a spot close enough to see the dolphins, but far enough from the waves that your blanket wouldn't get wet. Nothing ruined a date like the tide coming in.

Spending time with his niece was more important than any date. Brad knew that now. After years of chasing women and being away from his family, he was finally ready to settle down.

The thought startled him. What woman would want to start a life with him? His reputation as a heartbreaker had followed him back to Sunset Cove. It was his own fault, of course. He'd been breaking hearts and dumping girls long before he graduated from Sunset Cove High School.

Cheerful Sophia pulled Brad from his glum thoughts. She flung herself onto the blanket and popped open the pizza box, pulling out a cheesy slice. "I'm starving. We didn't have time for a snack at school today."

Brad grabbed his own slice and slid it onto a paper plate. "What did you do today?"

"We did math and spelling. I got to read a book in class, too. I like to read."

"That sounds like fun. What else did you do?"

She wrinkled her nose and nibbled another bite of pizza. "We had art class. I like art, but I had to share my paint with Caleb. He makes a mess."

"Boys are good at making messes. But I wouldn't talk. I've seen the messes you can make!"

That made Sophia giggle. She spent a moment watching the sun sink lower in the sky, then jumped up. "I'm done eating. I'm gonna look for shells before it gets dark."

Brad watched his niece as she combed the beach. After a few minutes, she ran back to the blanket with a shout.

Sophia grinned and held out a clam shell. "It's perfect! I'm saving it for the baby's room."

Brad's eyes darted from the shell to his niece's face. "What baby?"

"Well, there's no baby yet," she explained. "But I think there will be soon. I heard Mom and Dad talking about it last night when they thought I was sleeping. They want a baby. I hope it's a baby sister! I'm going to find her more shells."

Sophia dropped her first shell on the blanket and darted back to the water.

A baby, Brad thought. *A niece or nephew that I can watch grow up.* The idea made him surprisingly happy. Sophia was amazing, but he'd missed so much of her childhood. She'd make a good big sister, too.

Brad didn't know what he would have done without his little sister. Avery had given him a reason to keep moving forward after their parents died. They'd moved to Sunset Cove to live with their grandfather, but it hadn't been the same. While the rest of their friends were surrounded by aunts, uncles, and cousins, they'd only had Grandpa.

He wondered if Sophia wanted cousins. Brad wasn't sure if kids were in the cards for him. Not with his dating history. He didn't think he'd ever be lucky enough to start a family. For now, he'd soak up every minute that he could with his sister and her children.

Chapter Seven

Brook

BROOK SNAGGED ONE OF the last empty chairs at the Kindness Committee meeting. She was running late, as usual. There were never enough hours in the day. First, her shipment of supplies had been late; then a customer had walked into the shop as she prepared to lock up.

It seemed to never end, but that was okay. Life was boring if it became too predictable. She liked the changes, the flow, the people who had a special request. There weren't many tourists now, but requests were ramping up for the holiday. She had five orders so far for Valentine's Day cakes. Tourists would flood the town soon, eager to celebrate St. Valentine with their loved one in the small beach town.

Brook leaned across the table to talk to Avery. "Did you get everything done this week?"

Avery grinned. "We got the license. The final dress fitting is scheduled, and we ordered food for the reception. Our wedding party numbers are skewed now, but..."

"What do you mean?"

"Just a small change. I asked Brad to stand with me. Grant was happy to have him as a groomsman, but my brother belongs on my side." Avery beamed. "I'm glad we all get along. It's going to be a wonderful wedding."

Brook tilted her head in confusion. Stand with the bride? What did Avery mean? Brook opened her mouth to ask more questions, but she was interrupted as the door to the conference room banged open.

Brad strode into the room and placed a hand on the last empty chair—the chair next to Brook. He smiled down at her. "Is this seat taken?"

Brook tried to scan the room discreetly, searching for another empty chair. There weren't any.

She hadn't known Brad was joining the Kindness Committee. Now here he was, asking to sit next to her. Brook sighed and tried to paste a smile on her face. "It's all yours. Do you want me to trade with Avery? The two of you can sit together."

Brad sat down and spread out his notebook and pens, shaking his head. "This is fine. Unless you don't want to sit next to me. We've spent a lot of time together this week."

She rolled her eyes. "We grew up together, remember? It's fine. I'm immune to your charms."

Brad burst out laughing. "Of course you are. It's a good thing, too. We'll need to work together to support Avery during the wedding."

"What do you mean?" Brook glanced between Avery and her brother. "Avery said there was a change. You walked in before she could explain."

Avery leaned toward them and grinned. "Brad is going to be a bridesman! You'll both stand on my side at the altar and help me get ready that morning."

Brad raised an eyebrow. "You said nothing about getting ready. I'm not helping with the garter."

Brook snorted. She hadn't given much thought to the morning before the wedding. It could be awkward having a guy there, though.

She considered talking some sense into Avery, then looked at her friend across the table. Avery beamed back at her. She didn't have the heart to argue with her friend. If a bridesman made her happy, then that's what Avery would get.

Brook fidgeted with her pen as she mentally walked through the various scenarios. The bridesmaids helped with the bridal shower and the morning of the wedding. She held back a giggle at the thought of Brad juggling boxes of lacy nightgowns during a shower. It was a shame Avery had asked for no gifts.

Brook smoothed the laughter off her face and turned to Brad. She smiled sweetly. "I hope you fit into a bridesmaid's dress."

Brad waved off her concern and grinned. "Nah, Avery wouldn't do that to me. I'll wear a tux like the other guys." He winked at Brook, making her heart beat faster. "You're just jealous. I get to wear pants at the wedding, and you're stuck in a dress."

Brook stared at him, dumbfounded. How did he *do* that? One wink and her mind went blank. She tried to bring herself back to the conversation. Instead, she pictured how handsome Brad would look in a tux. She'd have a better view if he stood on the girls' side.

Get it together, she scolded herself. *He's a serial dater afraid of commitment. You've met enough of his type. Even if he is the best kisser...*

Brook was saved from that thought by the Kindness Committee's leader.

Pastor Rick Harris had founded the Kindness Committee last year. He'd wanted to help the people in need in Sunset Cove.

So far, it was working. The group had raised thousands of dollars. Every child at Sunset Cove Elementary School now had a warm winter coat that fit. These same kids had food in their bellies every weekend thanks to a new "Saturday Supper" book bag program. The local pantry was expanding their reach thanks to the

Kindness Committee, too. They'd used a Kindness gift to buy a new freezer and refill their emergency pantry.

More importantly, Pastor Rick was creating a network of helpers willing to donate their time. Grant had used his construction company's supplies to build a handicapped ramp and fix an elderly man's leaking roof. Brook had donated a cake to surprise a little girl coming home after chemotherapy.

She tried to pay attention to the pastor's prayer as he opened the meeting, but couldn't stop herself from thinking about that little girl. Brook could still picture her biting into the rich layers of frosting and vanilla cake, her parents hovering to make sure she didn't get icing in her wig.

The parents had later explained that the cake was a real blessing, especially since the girl hadn't been able to eat much in the hospital. She was finally getting her sense of taste back.

I should drop off another cake soon. Or maybe some cupcakes or cookies...

Her attention snapped back to the meeting when Pastor Rick cleared his throat and called Brook's name. "Sorry, what was that?"

The pastor stood next to Brook and smiled kindly. "I asked how your renovations were going. Are you shutting down, or will you stay open?"

"Oh! Umm, we'll be closed to customers for a bit after Valentine's Day. We're remodeling the kitchen first, but it's mostly moving new appliances into place."

Pastor Rick nodded and hummed in agreement. "I hope the project goes smoothly. The church's kitchen is available if you need it."

The thoughtful suggestion touched Brook. That was Pastor Rick—always thinking of his community members. He helped others and inspired people to do their best.

Pastor Rick turned to the group and continued speaking. "We've hit the slow season between Christmas and spring. There won't be as much to do right now, but please continue to keep Sunset Cove's neediest residents in your prayers. Our priority for the winter is making sure everyone in town has warm clothes and a roof over their heads. Does anyone have an update?"

Avery raised her hand. When the pastor nodded, she gestured for Grant to stand with her. "We have an update. As you all know, we're getting married."

The room erupted into cheers and clapping. Brook let out a whistle. Everyone had watched the couple dance around each other last fall, unwilling to admit that they were falling in love. They were thrilled to see Avery and Grant find their "happily ever after."

Grant raised his hands and gestured for silence. "We all know that the Kindness Committee played a role in our marriage. You gave us a purpose and pushed us together. Sometimes it wasn't a very subtle push, either." He gave Pastor Rick a side eye, then grinned. "We're grateful for everything you've done. In return, we'd like to repay your kindness in two ways. First, you're all invited to the wedding. It's nothing big, just a simple ceremony at Grace Lutheran. We'll have lunch in the community room afterwards."

"It's only fitting," Avery added. "We started our new life together in that room, during the community carnival."

Brook wiped away a tear as the couple continued sharing their plans. As a bridesmaid, she'd known where the wedding was going to take place, but she hadn't connected the dots. Avery was right. They really had started their lives together in that room. Her friend had struggled with the choice of committing to Grant or leaving Sunset Cove for good. In the end, she'd taken a leap of faith and found everything she needed in the town—including Grant.

Grant continued, gesturing to Pastor Rick. "We're grateful for what the Kindness Committee has done for us, and for this town.

To help pay back some of that kindness, we're asking people to skip the wedding gifts and donate to the Kindness fund instead."

Pastor Rick walked over to Grant and slapped him on the back. "That is very generous, my friend. Thank you. We're grateful for the support."

Grant pulled the pastor into a hug, giving the tall man a squeeze. "Sir, we wouldn't be here without you. It's the least we can do."

Pastor Rick hugged Grant back, then walked to the front of the room. "What a wonderful surprise!" The pastor seemed to choke up for a moment, overcome with emotions. "The greatest gift we can give is love. It's an honor to work with all of you."

He paused, taking a drink of water as he pulled himself back together. "Does anyone else have an update?" He gave people a few moments, then picked up a stack of papers. "If no one else has questions or updates, I'll share our spring project. Grace Lutheran has always sponsored an egg hunt for the church's youngest members. This year, I'd like to think bigger. Let's make this a Kindness project and invite all the children in town!"

He passed out a sheet of paper to each committee member, beaming as he walked. "I've always liked Easter egg hunts. And I love seeing the joy on each child's face as they open their candy. To keep costs low, I'll be asking community members to donate candy. There will also be a donation jar at the event, giving people a chance to continue our mission and donate to the Kindness Fund." He nodded to Avery. "Would you set up a table for the Clint Brown Kindness Fund? People seem especially eager to support your grandfather's legacy."

Avery nodded. "Absolutely. Tell me how I can help."

Pastor Rick cleared his throat. "The setup that day won't be a problem. You'll need a table for donations, and a small crew to hide and spread out buckets of eggs. My concern is filling the eggs. I'm aiming for five thousand."

Brad raised his hand, his eyebrows furrowed with confusion. He made a show of pointing to each person in the room as he silently counted off. "What's the problem? There are fifteen people here. If we work together, we can fill those eggs in no time."

Brook kicked him under the table. He looked at her and shrugged his shoulders. *What?* he mouthed. *It's fine.*

She shook her head, but it was too late. Pastor Rick clapped his hands and exclaimed, "Wonderful! I love your attitude. Can I put you in charge of the Easter eggs?"

Brook kicked him again, but Brad just smiled. "Sure. I don't mind. How much work can it be?"

Chapter Eight

Brad

BRAD WALKED TO THE parking lot with his friends after the meeting. He unlocked his car, then turned to stay goodbye to his sister.

She rounded on him with a look of horror on her face. "Have you ever filled five thousand eggs? I helped with Sophia's Easter egg hunt last year. It was *horrible*. No one wanted to help, and it took hours. My hands were cramping for days."

He stepped back in surprise, his hands held up in surrender. "How hard can it be? You open the egg and put a piece of candy in it. It won't take long if we have enough people."

Avery threw her head back and howled with laughter. "You don't understand. No one volunteers for these things." She gestured toward Brook and Grant, who hovered uncertainly while the siblings argued. "This is it. These are your volunteers. I'd be surprised if anyone else helps."

Brad's eyes widened. He looked over Avery's shoulder and watched the rest of the Kindness Committee members walk through the parking lot. Was it his imagination, or were they all avoiding eye contact?

He gulped. What had he gotten himself into? It was too late now, though. At least he had a few weeks to prepare for the egg hunt. They could start now and work a little every week. He'd put up flyers asking for donations.

His sister shook her head as she climbed into Grant's truck, but Grant seemed less worried. "It's okay. We've got your back. We'll recruit a few friends, too." Grant brightened at the idea and opened his truck door. "The Kindness Committee can always use new members. We'll make this fun."

That thought made Brad feel better. Between the four of them, they would rally enough people to help. Everything would be fine.

Besides, they'd faced bigger challenges. It wasn't long ago that he was trying to save their childhood home from tax sale. He'd worked with Avery on that, too. They were stronger together.

"See? No problem. Grant said it would be fun." Brad gave Brook what he hoped was a charming smile. "We'll find enough help."

Brook snorted as she pulled her car keys out of her jacket. "Grant's idea of a good time is a work party with saws and sandwiches. His standards are pretty low. You'll see. This is going to take forever." She rolled her eyes upward, mouthing numbers as if she was counting. "I'll ask Emma, Kerry and Rachel. They're not on the Kindness Committee, but they helped with our last fundraiser."

Brad nodded, feeling a bit of his confidence fade away. He was trying to show people he was a better person, more trustworthy—and he already needed saving. "Thanks. I should have listened when you tried to stop me."

Brook shoved her keys back into her pocket and crossed her arms. "Look, we'll help you. But there's a problem. Between the wedding, my bakery, and the egg hunt, we'll spend a lot of time together. I need to get something straight."

Brad mirrored her stance, shifting until his feet were apart and his arms crossed. "I'm listening. What's the problem?"

"I know we agreed to be friends, and I don't want things to be weird between us. But I can't watch you walk away from all these commitments. People will get hurt." *People like me,* she thought. "How long do you plan to stick around this time?"

Her question hit Brad like the stab of a knife. It was clear she still didn't trust him. Not completely, anyway. "Grant's looking to make me a foreman on his team. I'm hoping he plans to keep me for the long-term. I'm looking for an apartment right now."

Brook looked doubtful, but nodded. "We'll see how long you stay. But I've got rules. No flirting. Just business."

Brook's words hurt, but Brad knew he'd deserved them. It would take time to overcome his reputation. He hoped that if he stayed in town for a while, people would realize he'd changed. He wasn't the impulsive, carefree guy that he used to be. Coming back to Sunset Cove made him realize how foolish he'd been. When he looked at his sister and Grant, he wanted what they'd found—stability and a family.

He wouldn't get that from Brook; she didn't even trust him enough to try. So instead of arguing about her rules, he held up his hands. "Sounds fair. All work, no flirting." He gave her a little wave goodbye. "I'll see you tomorrow."

"What are we doing tomorrow?"

"We're going over the final plans for the kitchen, remember? Then we've got a dress fitting together. Avery asked to meet her there. We'll see if my tux can match the dresses better. See you later, bridesmaid."

He gave her a small smile and climbed into his truck, then slammed the door. He let out a breath as Brook did the same, and watched her drive away.

Chapter Nine

Brook

Brook watched with amusement as Brad settled himself into the pink, cushioned chair at Sunset Bridal. She hadn't expected him to show up for the dress fittings, but he'd promised Avery that he would be there. He was pretty good at keeping promises to his sister, she noted.

The other bridesmaids were in the dressing rooms, trying on their dresses one last time before the wedding. The only person missing was the bride.

Brook checked her phone for missed messages. As maid of honor, she'd let Avery talk her into leaving the bakery early to set up the dress fittings. Avery had promised to close the shop and get to their appointment on time.

No messages on her phone. She looked over at Brad, who was flipping through a bridal magazine. "Have you heard from your sister?"

"Not since this morning. She'll be here. What color are the flowers?"

"They're pink, to match our dresses." Brook watched with annoyance as Brad continued to flip through the magazine, examining each picture. "Aren't you worried about Avery? She's never late."

He sighed and closed the magazine, then turned his attention to Brook. "No, my sister's never late. But you're late all the time.

She probably got held up with a customer. You know how people come in at the last minute."

Brook grunted and crossed her arms snug across her body, settling deeper in her chair. As much as she hated to admit it, he had a point. Brook was only on time today because Avery was watching the store.

Some bridesmaid she was, letting the bride be late to her own dress fitting. She pulled out her phone again, determined to call Avery and tell her to close the store *right now*, customers or not.

Her finger was hovering over the call button when the door burst open.

Avery rushed into the room. "Sorry I'm late! Two customers came in at closing time. They were arguing over the last cupcakes. I talked them into sharing the cupcakes and a few muffins, and they both left happy." She gave Brook a wide grin as she shrugged off her coat. "How are things here?"

Brook jerked her head toward the dressing rooms. "Emma, Kerry and Rachel are trying on their dresses now. They should be out any minute."

Avery dropped into the overstuffed chair next to her brother and nodded. "I can't wait to see the dresses. We've got the guys in light gray tuxes, and the girls in soft pink. We just need to help Brad blend in on the girl's side."

He wiggled his eyebrows and gave Brook an amused look as he closed the magazine. "That's why I'm here. Trying to fit in with the girls."

Avery let out a giggle and elbowed Brad in the ribs. "He's such a good sport."

Brook shook her head and grinned. She'd never seen Avery so lighthearted.

Even Brad looked happier than she'd seen him in years. He moved over to close the gap between himself and Avery, leaning in to discuss something with his sister. It was great to see them together. It felt like high school, when they'd meet at the Brown house to make brownies or cupcakes. Brad had rarely missed a baking session, even after he'd left for college. He was always there to keep her company—and grab the first samples, fresh out of the oven. Until their first failed date, of course.

Determined to keep the mood light, Brook pushed that thought away and stood up. It was time to finish trying on dresses. "Should I get dressed, or do you want me to wait until the end?"

"Why don't you get dressed?" Avery glanced at Brad, then peeked past Brook's shoulder toward the dressing rooms. "It doesn't look like anyone else is done yet. We'll get the bridesmaids taken care of. Brad and I can talk about his tux alterations while we wait. No one says the bride has to try her dress on first."

Brook laughed at Avery's comment. Avery certainly wasn't a Bridezilla. She seemed to care more about the wedding party than herself.

Brook snagged the last dressing room and shimmied into her bridesmaid's dress. Avery's offer to let her get dressed first shouldn't surprise her. She'd always known Avery was kind-hearted. As she struggled to reach the zipper of her dress, she wondered why she couldn't give Brad the same benefit of the doubt. He wasn't a bad guy—unless you were his girlfriend.

As each day passed, she was finding it easier to forgive Brad for what he'd done. He'd hurt her, of course. The least he could have done was give her closure: a phone call, or even a text, saying he wasn't interested. But part of this was her fault, too. She could've asked Avery for his number, or visited the house when he was in town. Instead, she'd kept her head down and worked just as hard to avoid him.

They'd been kids when they dated. She should have known better, though. Brad wasn't known for long-term commitments. Best to stick to the rules now. No dating, no flirting. Just friends.

She sighed, abandoning her efforts to psychoanalyze their relationship, and also her attempts to reach the dress zipper on her own. Brook stepped into the hallway, where the rest of the bridesmaids chatted quietly as the seamstress checked each dress.

Emma, her quietest friend and the single mom in the group, noticed Brook first. "Turn around. Let me zip you up. You'd have to be a contortionist to close these dresses on your own."

"Thanks. They're gorgeous dresses once they're on, though." Brook smiled at her quietest friend and stepped away. With the zipper fastened, the dress fit perfectly. They'd done a great job with the alterations.

Kerry, the boldest friend in their group, gave the rest of them a wicked grin. "We'll need help getting out of these dresses, too. It's a shame we're all single. Maybe some nice-looking guys at the wedding can help us. I hear Brad's still available."

Brook tried to hide her laugh by breaking into a coughing fit. Her friends weren't fooled.

"What's so funny?" Kerry asked. "Brad's the most attractive man to move to Sunset Cove in years. We'd be fools if one of us didn't make a move."

Brook shook her head, motioning for Kerry to keep her voice down. "First, he's right outside. Be quiet. Second, you don't know Brad. He doesn't do relationships. He's more of a single-date kind of guy."

"I'd be okay with one date." Kerry wiggled her eyebrows. "I'm free the day after the wedding. I'll have to check his calendar, though."

Brook sighed. Kerry was impossible. She took pride in being single, but was the first to make jokes about the single guys in town. Kerry might sing a different tune if she'd known Brad in high school.

Instead of starting an argument, Brook reached for the door handle. "My dress fits. I'm going to check in with Avery." The seamstress nodded, then turned back to adjusting Kerry's dress.

When Brook stepped out of the dressing area, Brad was deep in conversation with the shop owner. They leaned over a book of fabric samples.

"This is a close match. Let's use this pink, maybe in a handkerchief?" Brad glanced at Avery, who nodded. "I want it to be bold. The people in the back row should be able to see it."

"A matching pink pocket square, with a pointed fold to show as much color as possible. Would that work?" the shop owner asked. "The florist is already matching the boutonnieres to the ladies' bouquets, so the flowers won't be a problem. That gives you two pops of pink color."

Avery nodded, then pulled out her phone as it started vibrating. "It's perfect. Sorry, I've got to take this. Grant's calling."

Brad hummed in agreement as the shop owner closed the fabric book. "She's right. It is perfect. Thanks for working with us. I want Avery's day to be as beautiful as possible."

"You've put some thought into this," Brook said, joining Brad as he settled into the overstuffed chair.

Brad blinked as he took in Brook's maid of honor dress, with its sweetheart top and ruffled bottom. "You look beautiful." He stared at her for a moment, then cleared his throat. "But yeah, I've thought a lot about fitting in with the bridesmaids. This is important to her. We drifted apart after she got married the first time. I'd like to make it up to her."

Brook smiled and reached over to squeeze his hand. "Don't worry. Grant won't let that happen again." She smiled at him, then looked down at their hands. They were still linked. Brook took a step backward and let their hands drop. "Anyway, it's nice of you to stand up for your sister, even if it means wearing pink." Brook paused, guilt flooding her as she considered how long she'd held a grudge against Brad. She hadn't treated him well since he'd moved back to town. "You've changed a lot since high school. We need to put the past behind us."

"No more rules? Just two friends, living in the same town and working together."

Brook smiled at Brad. "Just friends," she agreed. "The no-flirting rule still stands, though."

Avery walked back into the bridal shop. "Sorry, that was Grant. He had an update on the bakery's renovations." Brook tried to focus as Avery spoke. Something about building materials being rush-ordered, and a storm headed toward New Jersey. It was probably important, but Brook still had trouble focusing on the conversation.

She'd gotten what she asked for. She was friends with Brad again. No strings, no more weird conversations about the past.

So why did she feel so empty inside?

Chapter Ten

Brook

Seaside Cupcakes' kitchen had never felt so crowded.

It was a Monday, which meant the bakery was closed to customers. Brook and Avery stood wedged in one corner of the kitchen, going over inventory and making plans for the next few weeks. Brook was shocked to realize how much she depended on Avery. It would be tricky finding time to do everything while her friend took time off for the wedding.

I can make this work, Brook reminded herself. *I ran this shop alone for years. Besides, we'll be closed for a few days while the guys put in my new oven and countertops.*

The noise in the kitchen wasn't helping her focus. The renovations had already begun—Brad and Grant were attempting to pull out her second stove to make room for a new double oven.

Judging by the muttering and loud noises, it wasn't going well.

"You know, I never appreciated how large this stove is," Brad panted. "We could put the new ovens on top of it. Then she'd have three ovens."

Grant rolled his eyes and adjusted the protective mats he'd put under and in front of the stove. "This is your first commercial kitchen, isn't it? Everything is bigger and heavier in a restaurant. We're almost done, though. A few more inches and we can start using the appliance dolly."

But Brad had already stopped listening to Grant. Instead, he walked across the kitchen to turn up the radio they'd left playing for background noise.

The New Jersey coast will face the worst of this weekend's storm. Nicknamed "Travis," this Nor'easter storm will make landfall on Friday morning, bringing a significant amount of rain before turning to snow. Heavy wind is expected.

A coastal flood advisory has been issued for Sunset County. Stay tuned for more updates on the impending storm.

Brook groaned as Brad turned down the volume on the radio. Avery and Grant's wedding was this weekend. The last thing they needed was a flood.

Grant turned to her and shrugged. "Don't worry about it yet. We've dealt with flooding before. Besides, the church is on higher ground. Even coastal flooding can't reach it."

"It's taken me ten years to marry this man. We won't let a storm stop us," Avery assured her. She stood up and walked over to Grant for a kiss. "Besides, it's good luck if it rains on your wedding day."

Brook sighed and drifted over to the walk-in fridge. She needed to keep her mind busy. She couldn't bake now, not with everyone stuffed into the kitchen. But she could whip up some cannoli dip after they left. She'd wrap it up and put it out tomorrow. The sweet treat was always a crowd pleaser and made a great accompaniment to her chocolate chip cookies.

Besides, a bit of the creamy dip might soothe her frazzled nerves.

She confirmed that there was enough whipping cream in the fridge, then closed the door and backed up. But instead of backing into the space between the refrigerator and counter, she hit a solid wall of muscle.

Brad's arms reached out to steady her as she wobbled from the collision. "Easy, there. Space is a little tight right now."

"Sorry about that," she mumbled. "There's no room with everyone in here."

"We're leaving soon. The oven's out, and Grant is pulling the truck around. The tricky part will be when we install the new appliances."

Brook grimaced as she thought about the next steps. After the wedding, Brad and Nick would install her new double oven and replace the countertops. She hated the idea of closing for even a few days.

"We'll work as quickly as possible," Brad reassured her. "You'll be open and working in your new kitchen before you know it."

Brook had dreamed of the changes she'd make to this kitchen for ages, long before she'd purchased the building. She'd jumped at the chance to buy the space when her catering boss retired. It had taken years to save up the money to remodel.

Still, Brook knew she should be grateful. Grant Construction had a lengthy waiting list for new projects. She was fortunate her friend could fit the kitchen into his schedule. With that thought in mind, she turned to face Grant. "Thanks again for doing this. I know you're busy."

"That's an understatement." Grant laughed and jerked his head in Brad's direction. "But if you're going to thank someone, thank Brad. You'd be waiting until summer if he hadn't joined the crew. We might be friends, but I won't install a kitchen during my honeymoon."

The four of them laughed at his comment. The wedding and falling in love had made Grant's life busier. But while Brook understood how overwhelmed Grant felt, she knew he wouldn't change anything.

A spark of jealousy struck her, making Brook blink in surprise. She was happy for her friends, of course. But she hadn't felt jealous of them before. She was content being single and spending all of her hours at the bakery. Wasn't she?

As the men finished loading the stove and wheeled it out the door, Avery jumped up in surprise. "The food! I almost forgot about lunch."

"Don't worry, I would have reminded you." Brad patted his stomach and grinned. "I'll never turn down lunch at Seaside Cupcakes."

Avery rushed over to the refrigerator and pulled out a plate of sandwiches and homemade iced tea. She rolled her eyes at her brother. "We don't even serve lunch at Seaside Cupcakes, and you know it."

Brad just laughed and pushed the kitchen door open, holding it as his friends walked through.

Brook felt another pang of jealousy as she watched Grant pull out a chair for Avery. What was wrong with her? Sure, her last date hadn't even made it to dinner. That didn't mean she couldn't be excited for her best friend's wedding.

Still, it had been a long time since a man pulled out a chair for her. She sighed and reached for her own seat, but stopped when she realized Brad's hand was already there.

"Sorry. Just being polite," he said. Brad pulled out the chair and gestured for her to sit down.

Brook blushed and nodded, then sat down in the chair. The four friends chatted while they devoured the plate of sandwiches and iced tea, discussing the wedding and the upcoming storm. But Brook couldn't help but let her mind wander. Brad seemed different, somehow. Kinder, and more mature.

She firmly pushed aside any ideas about them being together. Sure, he'd matured. But they'd already agreed to be nothing more than friends.

No games, no flirting, no broken promises. Just friends.

Chapter Eleven

Brad

BRAD SAT WITH HIS sister in their lawyer's office the next morning, signing the paperwork that would close their grandfather's estate.

They'd been working toward this day for a long time. Brad hadn't realized closing an estate was so complicated. He'd had a front-row seat to every one of his grandfather's bills and accounts.

Brad felt a huge weight lift off his shoulders as he signed the last piece of paper, set down the pen, and handed the stack of documents to their lawyer, Daniel Rawler. Being his grandfather's executor was one of the most difficult things he'd ever done. It was like throwing salt on a wound—being forced to take care of a family member's last responsibilities while you grieve their loss.

He gave the lawyer a thin smile, thinking of the work it had taken to get here. "That's it? We're done with the estate?"

"I'm here if you need legal advice. For now, our work is done." Daniel closed the folder on his desk. "The estate is settled. You and your sister own the house. I hear there's a wedding planned, too. Congratulations!"

Avery grinned. "Thanks. We'd love if you could make it. I know you were close to our grandfather."

"That reminds me!" Daniel dug through his desk and pulled out the wedding invitation. "I never sent back my RSVP, but I'll be there. If it's not too late, of course."

"Of course it isn't. We're not having a formal sit-down dinner. The more, the merrier." Avery beamed at the lawyer as she stood up and shrugged on her coat. "Thank you again for helping us move forward. I need to get back to work. It's my last day. Brook's waiting for me—we're stocking up on her customers' favorites to sell after the wedding."

Brad stood up with his sister, walking over to hold the door open for her. "What's Brook saying about the mess?"

"She's making the best of it. She's stressed about the expansion, though. I'm worried she's stretching herself too thin."

Brad nodded. "She puts in a lot of hours. I've been trying to finish my planning when she's not there, but she's always working."

"I've never seen her take a day off. If she doesn't work, the bakery doesn't open. That's a lot of pressure on one person. Speaking of the bakery, I've got to get back." Avery gave her brother a hug and started the short walk back to work.

Brad watched his sister leave and thought about her words. The bakery's expansion would let them serve more customers, but how would that help? Brook could barely keep up as it was. She started work before the sun rose, and stayed long after the store closed to prep for the next morning.

Brad hadn't realized how hard it was to build a business. Grant's construction company had a small crew. He'd only hired Brad and one other worker, but every man counted in a construction crew. A second foreman would make a big difference, too.

Brad wished that Brook would hire more people, too—if only to give herself a break. He gave the lawyer one last nod as he pulled on his own coat. "Thank you again, sir. It's been nice working with you." Brad held out his hand, and Daniel gave him a firm handshake.

"Now that the estate's settled, what are your plans? You mentioned staying in Sunset Cove until the house title was transferred."

Brad shoved his hands into his coat pocket, considering his next words. "I'll be around for a while. Not in Grandpa's house—it's going to be crowded once Grant moves in. I'm looking for an apartment."

"That makes sense. The new family will need some space. I'm glad to hear you're staying, though."

"It was a tough decision," Brad admitted. "We only came to Sunset Cove after my parents died. There were lots of bad memories here, you know? But Grant needs a new foreman, and he treats me a lot better than my old boss. I like spending time with my sister's family, too. It's fun being an uncle. I'm hoping to set down some roots in town."

"Sunset Cove is a great place to grow roots," the lawyer agreed. He checked that all of their paperwork was together, then turned around to put the folder into a filing cabinet behind his desk. "You've earned quite a reputation, though. You seem like a nice enough guy, but I've been told to keep my granddaughters away from you." Daniel turned back to face Brad, his eyebrows raised. "Is there truth in that statement?"

Brad groaned and shook his head. *Can't I leave the past behind me?* he wondered. "I've never been into commitment. That changed when I came home. I'm not looking to get married or anything right now, but I want what my sister's found—stability, and a partner. Hopefully, I'll find that for myself one day, sir. It just needs to be the right person at the right time."

"Those are wise words, young man. No reason to rush. You've got your whole life ahead of you."

Brad walked out of the lawyer's office with a frown. He knew Daniel's words were true. But unless he overcame his reputation,

Brad was worried he might spend the rest of his life alone. The thought made his stomach twist.

He didn't want to have a different girl on his arm each week. Still, he hadn't committed to a long-term relationship since... never. Brad tried to remember a relationship that had lasted for more than a week or two. He couldn't.

Time to put the brakes on dating. Focus on his sister and niece. There was lots to get done in the next few months: help with the wedding, find an apartment, and get settled into a new neighborhood. Finish the work at the bakery and learn more about becoming a foreman.

Brad had the rest of his life to find the right woman.

Chapter Twelve

Brook

LATER THAT NIGHT, BROOK rushed through the parking lot at Grace Lutheran Church. The outer edge of the storm had arrived, bringing downpours and heavy wind.

Brook remained cheerful as she yanked open the door to the church's community hall, juggling an umbrella and a box of centerpiece supplies. At least it wasn't snowing. Sure, the rain might cause flooding. But snow was slippery and needed to be shoveled.

She wrinkled her nose. Shoveling snow was one of her least favorite things to do. They didn't get many snow storms so close to the Atlantic Ocean. When it did snow, it made a *mess*.

Emma rushed toward Brook. "There you are! The school buses are running behind, so Avery and Rachel aren't here yet. How are the roads?" She took the box from Brook's arms, then stepped back as Brook brushed off the rain clinging to her coat.

"They're not terrible. I heard on the radio that there's flooding near the marina. That happens with heavy storms, though. The main roads are still clear." Brook hung up her coat and propped her umbrella in the stand, letting both drip onto the mat underneath. The umbrella hadn't helped much. Wind was blowing the rain everywhere.

Brad sauntered up to the women and offered to take the box from Emma. "This is some storm. It's been a long time since I lived in Sunset Cove. I forgot how fierce a Nor'easter can be along the coast." He moved the box to the table and emptied its contents, pulling out twinkle lights, artificial flowers, and a dozen vases. "Is this going to be enough? How many tables are there?"

Brook grinned and walked over to the supply closet, pulling out another large box. "We're fine. I've been bringing supplies over all week. We would have started sooner, but the battery-operated lights got lost in the mail."

She pulled a vase out of the box, then showed them how to wind lights around the flower stems and into the flowers themselves. She tucked the on/off switch near the top and turned on the lights.

"Very pretty!" Emma sighed. "Brook, you're so creative."

Brad grinned at the little twinkling bulbs. "We're set if the power goes out, too. Plenty of light during the storm."

Brook turned to glare at him. "Not funny. This weekend is going to be perfect. Why are you here, anyway? I didn't think you'd want to help with the centerpieces."

"My sister invited me. I'm part of the bridal party, remember? Besides, you don't need me to work on centerpieces. I can be useful in other ways." Brad flexed his muscles, then picked up two long tables resting against the wall. He carried them to the far side of the room. "I saw the seating plan. I'll get these tables set up while you work on the centerpieces."

Yikes. Brook knew how heavy those tables were. She'd struggled to move one by herself, and Brad could carry two at a time.

"Every wedding should have a bridesman," Kerry murmured as she reached for a string of lights. "I'm all about girl power, but it's nice to have someone to move the furniture."

Kerry had a point. Brad would save them a lot of time. The four bridesmaids sat in the corner, wrapping strands of lights around flower stems and filling the table with centerpieces. Brad hustled around the room, setting up tables and covering each one with a white tablecloth.

Emma glanced out the window at the pouring rain, a wrinkle of worry settling on her forehead. "Has anyone checked the weather? This will clear up by Saturday, right?"

Kerry snorted. "Not likely. Is this your first Nor'easter? The storm hasn't even hit us yet. This is mother nature's warning that a storm's coming."

"I've never heard of a Nor'Easter. Are they bad?" Emma's eyes widened.

Brook swatted Kerry's arm and tried to give Emma a reassuring look. "It's a storm that travels up the east coast. They can bring heavy snow or rain. Right now, the weatherman says we'll get a lot of rain and wind. We've gotten through worse."

"The weatherman's not sure what's going to happen," Kerry added helpfully. "If it gets colder, we could get a lot of snow. If it stays warmer, we'll get more rain and flooding."

"Is flooding a problem? We live by the ocean. Won't all the water go out to sea?" Emma argued, watching the rain pound against the windows.

The other friends laughed. Emma had moved from Ohio to Sunset Cove last year, and this was her first big storm. They'd been blessed with a mild fall and winter the previous year.

Brook took a deep breath and turned her attention to Emma. She didn't want to scare her friend, but there was no point in hiding the truth. Storms along the coast could turn bad, and quickly. Coverage of past storms would play on television for most of this week. "We've had flooding before. If the wind gets bad enough, it could make flooding worse. It's called a storm surge. The wind pushes the waves higher and higher until it increases the height of high tide. Then you've got flooding from the rain and snow, plus water from the ocean coming into town."

Emma set down her centerpiece with a whimper. "Does that happen often?"

"Storm surges don't happen very often, but when they do, they can cause a lot of damage," Brad said, walking over to pick up a vase and a fistful of flowers. "They're not expecting anything too serious from this storm. It's hard to predict weather near the ocean, though. It's nothing like living in the middle of the country. You've got the ocean currents and the warmer air over the ocean mixing and creating chaos. It makes things a lot less predictable."

Brook closed her eyes, feeling guilty for bringing up the worst possible outcomes. She nudged Brad with her elbow. "Stop it, you're scaring Emma. It's going to be fine. I've lived in Sunset Cove my entire life. We've evacuated once in thirty years. The odds of that happening this weekend are pretty low." She smiled at her friend and reached out to squeeze her hand. "We'll get through this storm. Hopefully, our biggest concern will be getting the cake here in one piece. I'm not sure how to deliver it with this wind!"

"Last winter wasn't like this." Emma looked doubtful, despite her friend's encouraging words. "We didn't have any snow. This feels bad."

Kerry grinned as she picked up another artificial flower and twisted it into the centerpiece. "Last winter was awesome. Above average temperatures and no snow. We sold houses all the way through January." Kerry worked at the bank and specialized in personal finance and business loans. She had a hand in nearly every house or business sold in Sunset Cove. "Think of this storm as your official winter welcome. Besides, it's the mayor's job to watch the weather. If it gets too dangerous, he'll evacuate the town. We'll be safe even if there's flooding."

But Brad stared at the window, letting his flowers sit loosely in his lap. "Let's keep our fingers crossed that the wedding happens with no problems. Worst-case scenario, we cut the reception short to get people home before the water rises too far. When it floods, it's usually the first block or two by the ocean. The church is on high ground, and our houses are far enough…" He turned to look at Brook, his eyes filled with concern. "Only the buildings by the boardwalk are at risk."

The windows rattled ominously as Brook slammed her centerpiece down on the table. She knew her bakery was a block from the ocean. No reminders needed. "Nothing's going to happen. Now let's get these centerpieces done. I've still got a wedding cake to bake."

She snatched another handful of flowers and string of lights, angrily weaving the lights between the plastic leaves and petals. Leave it to Brad to unlock her biggest worries. The bakery's building had only flooded once in her memory, a few years before it became the old catering storefront.

Back then, the building had housed a small takeout restaurant. Flooding had forced the restaurant to close at the start of tourist season. They reopened mid-season, but declared bankruptcy less than a year later.

She knew her building was at high risk of flooding. There wasn't much she could do about it.

The strength of ten bridesmen couldn't stop the ocean from flooding Sunset Cove.

Chapter Thirteen

Brad

THE NEXT DAY, BRAD sat in the parking lot outside Grace Lutheran Church. He watched the bare tree branches blow in the wind. The worst of the storm was nearly here.

The branches gave an ominous creak as they rubbed together. It had been years since he'd lived in a coastal town, but this storm had him on edge. It wasn't only because he wanted his little sister's wedding to be perfect. He had a bad feeling. There hadn't been a storm surge in Sunset Cove in years. That didn't mean one couldn't happen this week.

His biggest concern was Brook's bakery. If the tide flooded her neighborhood, she would be in big trouble.

Brad climbed out of his truck and dashed through the pouring rain. The rehearsal was tonight, but people rushed around the church with the urgency of a wedding day. That didn't surprise him. With the worst of the storm scheduled to hit during the wedding, everything needed to go smoothly tomorrow. There would be no simple runs across town for last-minute flowers in this rain.

He hung up his coat and went looking for Brook. He found her in the worship hall. As maid of honor, she was busy directing the rest of the bridesmaids as they tied flowers to each pew.

"Wonderful weather we're having. How can I help?" he asked.

"We're almost done here. You can find the pastor and the happy couple. We need to start the rehearsal soon." She turned away from Brad, then did a double-take. "What's with the pink shirt?" She laughed as she took in his light pink button-down shirt and matching tie. "It's a nice color on you, but I thought you'd save the pink clothes for tomorrow."

Brad shrugged and pulled at his neckline. He hated ties, but he'd wanted to make a good impression on Avery—and Brook, too. "Trying to fit in with the bridal party. It's strange being the only guy in a group of girls. Not that I'm complaining," he rushed to add. "It's what Avery wants."

Brook looked impressed at his response. "You look great. Let's call it a salmon shirt. Nothing strange about a guy wearing salmon." After Brad laughed and nodded, she reached up to turn him toward the back of the worship hall. "Now go find people. We can't have a rehearsal without the bride and groom."

Brad wandered around the church for a few minutes before finding Avery and Grant in the pastor's office. The three of them were studying a map of coastal highways and county roads.

"This is the safest evacuation route," Grant said, tracing his finger over the laptop screen. "It leads to the highway and straight away from the coast. But where would we go?"

"My friend's congregation will take us in. They can hold five hundred people in their main hall. That's most of the town." Pastor Rick looked at the couple. "Hopefully, it won't come to that. But it's good to have a backup plan."

Brad cleared his throat, causing them to jump. They all turned around to stare at Brad, their faces frozen in a mix of surprise and guilt.

Avery spoke first. "Brad! I didn't hear you come in. Is it time for the rehearsal?"

"We're ready to get started. Brook sent me to find you. Why are you making evacuation plans?"

"It's strictly a backup plan," Pastor Rick explained. "There's a cold front coming in tomorrow morning. It could cause snow and icy roads. Lots of wind, too. The mayor is expecting quite a mess."

"Snow and wind aren't a reason to evacuate. And even if there's flooding, it won't reach the church." Brad crossed his arms and stared at the pastor. "There's something you're not telling me."

Pastor Rick sighed. "I don't want to cause a panic, but the mayor is sending a warning out using our text alert system. This wind could cause problems. If there's a storm surge, the roads will be under water. Flooding and snow could cut us off from the rest of the county."

Brad stared at the wall, thinking. He'd agreed with Brook that extreme flooding wasn't likely. But if the mayor said they had to leave town, it was best to listen. He couldn't deny that the pastor's idea was a good one. Lots of people would need a place to go. It was better to plan for the worst and hope for the best. "What can I do?" he asked. "How can I help?"

The pastor nodded. "The mayor has his own ways of contacting the town. My Kindness Committee does, too. We'll encourage people to consider evacuating to my friend's church. He's gathering donations in case we need to feed a few hundred people. My biggest concern is the people who can't drive. Can I put you on the carpool list?"

Grant stepped forward. "Put both of us on the list. We can each help a few extra people evacuate."

The pastor added both of their names to a short list on his desk. "Not a word about this, to anyone. Let the mayor handle the official announcement. No need to start a panic. The mayor will encourage people to pack their bags. I'll call our congregation's shut-ins tonight to tell them the carpool plan. But for now, we've got a wedding rehearsal to get through. "

Brad looked from the pastor to his sister and frowned. "Shouldn't we postpone the wedding? We can push it back a few weeks. That's got to be an option."

"The storm could shift, or slow down. We can't let fear rule our lives," Avery argued. "We'll just move the wedding to the evacuation point if we have to."

"Move the whole wedding to a new town? That's crazy." Brad stared at his sister with wide eyes.

"It was my idea," the pastor interjected, holding up his hands to stop the budding argument. "Legally, I can marry them anywhere in New Jersey. I gave them the choice to postpone or move the wedding."

"I've waited half my life for someone like Avery," Grant said, smiling at his fiance. "A storm won't stop me from marrying her tomorrow."

Brad shook his head. "This is crazy, but okay. Let's pray the storm shifts and none of this matters."

As the four of them walked toward the church sanctuary, Grant pulled Brad aside. "I need a favor. If we have to evacuate, can I count on you to make sure Brook leaves town? She might try to stay behind."

"Why would she do that?"

"To save the bakery. It's her entire world. She won't leave without a fight."

Brad stared at his boss and friend. "Brook's a determined woman, but she can't stop the ocean from rising. There's nothing she can do if there's a flood."

Grant nodded grimly. "I know that. She'll try, though. Get her to leave, even if it means carrying her out of the building."

Brad prayed it wouldn't come to that. Brook wouldn't be happy if he forced her to leave. Still, Grant was right. It was important that they all stuck together and got everyone out of town safely.

·♥·♥·♥·♥·♥·

Despite the howling wind and the trees swaying outside the church's windows, the wedding rehearsal went smoothly. Brad practiced walking down the aisle with the bridesmaids. Sophia, the youngest member of the bridal party, was on her best behavior and only giggled twice.

Brad didn't start sweating until it was time to leave the church.

"We're lopsided," Brook said, counting the number of attendants on each side. "Not counting the flower girl, there are four men and four women. But we've got a bridesman, so there are five people on our side. What should we do?"

Grant eyed up the bride's side and shrugged. "Brook, walk with Brad. That will even up the numbers."

Brad looked up from his niece. He'd been deep in conversation about tonight's dinner plans. They were both hoping for chicken fingers. Brad nodded in agreement with Grant, then paused. "Wait. What am I agreeing to? I missed that."

"We don't have enough groomsmen to walk back up the aisle." Grant gestured toward the longer line next to his fiance. "I know you're standing on the bride's side, but you're a guy. Walk with a lady. Brook's standing right next to you, so walk with her."

Brad turned to Brook and frowned. How had he gone from standing next to Brook to being partnered with her? He'd convinced himself that he was content to be friends with Brook. He'd promised himself, and his sister, that things wouldn't get awkward.

This felt awkward.

To his surprise, Brook laughed and held out an arm. "Come on, it won't be that bad. One quick walk and we're done. Well, two walks. We'll have to do this again tomorrow, during the wedding."

"Don't forget the first dance at the reception," Grant called, his eyes alight with mischief. "Two walks and one slow dance. Can you handle it, Brad?"

We're just friends, Brad reminded himself. *Do this for your sister.* He said a short, silent prayer that he wouldn't make a fool out of himself or anyone else, then looped his arm through Brook's. "We can handle this."

They walked out of the church together, leading the rest of the bridal party. Pastor Rick followed to congratulate them all on a job well done.

Their next stop was the community hall, where a simple meal waited. Brad grinned as Sophia squealed in delight. She'd found the chicken fingers. His niece was so excited about the wedding. She knew her mom was happy and loved her new stepdad. The three of them glowed with excitement as they led their friends through the buffet table.

If the weather cooperated, it would be a beautiful wedding. Brad felt silly for worrying about whose arm he held as he walked up the church aisle.

He filled his plate with chicken fingers to make his niece smile, then added a burger and some fries. Avery had told him the rehearsal dinner's food would be simple. The Cove, an outdoor grill they'd all loved growing up, was trying to expand its business with a food truck and low-key catering. There were plenty of fancy restaurants in the surrounding towns. Nothing could beat The Cove's burgers and Sunset Sauce.

Brad sat down next to his niece and picked up a chicken finger. "I told you there'd be good food." The little girl nodded and dragged a fry through a mountain of ketchup.

Knowing that Sophia would stay focused on food for a while, he turned to the bride and groom. The two of them talked quietly, her head resting on his shoulder. Their food was untouched. Brad wondered what they were talking about. He hoped thoughts of an evacuation weren't ruining their day.

The smell of vanilla and a quiet voice startled Brad out of these thoughts.

"Can I sit here?" Brook asked. "Avery's taking some time off, so we need to coordinate schedules. Do you mind talking about work tonight?"

Brad looked up, surprised to find Brook standing next to him. Her perfume was like a punch straight to his gut. For a moment, he forgot that they'd agreed to be friends. For a moment, he flashed back to his college years. He was greeting Brook as he picked her up for their first date. The night was full of potential.

Brad shook his head, attempting to clear his thoughts. His sister's wedding vibes were rubbing off on him. Now wasn't the time to daydream about the past. He pushed out the chair next to him and nodded. "Have a seat. Let's brainstorm."

She sat in her chair and grabbed one fry from her plate, chewing as she thought. "With Avery gone, I'll be starting earlier to get my work done. Mornings won't be a great time to talk about the renovations. Can we push the work into the afternoon?"

Brad considered her request. He was supposed to be working on the bakery full-time. Still, there wasn't much left to do right now. They'd picked out most of the appliances, the new countertops and the cabinets. "I won't need to spend much time at the bakery next week," he admitted. "Until we're ready to tear out countertops and replace the oven, I can leave you in peace. I'll stop by one afternoon to finalize our plans."

While he thought this news would be a relief, Brook seemed disappointed. Maybe she'd looked forward to having company.

Brad had found their daily get-togethers oddly comfortable. It wasn't often that he worked on site with a business owner. It had been fun, though. And not because he'd gotten extra food out of the deal.

Avery must have overheard their conversation, because she glanced their way with a frown. "I hate leaving you with no help. We're not leaving for a honeymoon right now, just taking time for ourselves. Are you sure you don't want me to come in?"

Brook shook her head. "No way. You deserve a few days off. Start a routine with your new family. It's the slow season, anyway."

Grant looked from his wife to Brook. "We'll both be back to work soon. It's tough to be without help. Have you thought about hiring another person? Maybe someone at the high school who could work before school. Expanding my crew was the best thing I've done this year." He nodded toward Brad. "We might expand the crew even further this spring. I've already told Brad that I'm training him to be a foreman. Might need more workers to help him."

Brad grinned and leaned forward toward his boss. "I hope that's an official job offer. I've already called my boss out in Pittsburgh, to let him know I won't be back in the spring."

Grant reached out to shake Brad's hand. "Good to hear it. I'm looking forward to seeing you lead a crew of your own."

Avery glanced between her fiance and brother. "This is all wonderful. I'm proud of both of you. Can we focus on the wedding for one more day? We need to talk about the speech."

"Go ahead. Let's talk. What speech?" Brad picked up his burger, taking care not to let the ketchup drip onto his pink shirt.

"Traditionally, the maid of honor writes a speech for the reception." She looked at Brook, who nodded. "It's last minute, but it would mean a lot if Brad said something, too. Maybe you can work with Brook."

Brook started laughing. "If I didn't know better, I'd think you were pushing us together. First, we're standing next to each other at the wedding. Then we're walking and dancing together. Now you want us to write a speech."

Brad's heart pounded as he thought about Brook's words. She was right, of course. They'd been pushed together throughout the wedding preparations. It was getting harder and harder to play the "just friends" card.

But it didn't matter what he thought, or how worried he was about his sister's plans. Brad had a lot of big-brother duties to catch up on after their years apart. He'd do almost anything she asked.

He took a sip of soda, hoping to act casual as he waved off Brook's concerns. "Avery knows you're not interested. We won't have time to write the speech tomorrow morning, so why don't we get together tonight? I'm still staying at Avery's house."

Brook shook her head. "Come to my apartment. We'll have more space and quiet to focus."

The members of the wedding party soon drifted out of the church and toward their cars. As the two of them walked out together, Brook turned to Brad. "You're really staying?" She shook her head. "You said you would, but I still thought you'd be gone by spring. I never imagined you'd settle in Sunset Cove for good. You were just as eager as Avery to leave when we were kids."

Brad leaned against Brook's car as he considered what she'd said. "This town held a lot of bad memories," he reminded her. "We're lucky our grandfather was here to pick up the pieces after our parents died. Wish I hadn't been in such a hurry to leave. My parents' death messed us up."

Brook hesitated, then stepped forward and wrapped Brad in a hug. "You had to leave, but I'm glad you're back."

If Brad didn't know better, he'd think she was leaning a bit too close. As if she expected a kiss.

No, that couldn't be right. Kissing wasn't an option. Brook had been clear about that.

He gave her a hearty pat on the shoulder and jerked his chin toward her car. "I'll meet you at the bakery. We've got a speech to write."

Chapter Fourteen

Brook

Brook stood outside the bakery, pacing the sidewalk as she waited for Brad to arrive. She regretted inviting him back to her place. What had happened in the parking lot? She'd given him a hug, and suddenly they'd been leaning closer and closer together. He'd glanced at her lips, as if anticipating a kiss.

No kissing. No second chances. No way.

Only now she'd put them in the awkward spot of meeting in her apartment above the bakery, alone. Brook mentally beat herself up, wishing they'd agreed to meet anywhere else. The speech she'd started was on her phone—they could have stayed at the church, or gone to the ice cream shop. Anywhere but her apartment.

Too late now. Brad's truck pulled to the curb. He gave a little wave after he parked, then climbed out of the truck. He stuck his hands in his pockets, looking almost as nervous as she felt. "We've both got an early start tomorrow. Where should we do this?" Brad glanced through the bakery windows.

Brook could almost hear his thoughts: If they stayed in the bakery's booths, they'd be in plain sight of anyone who walked by. It was almost like being supervised.

She hesitated, then decided they were overthinking things. They were just friends. No reason not to let a friend into her apartment. She gestured toward the steps outside the bakery. "Upstairs is fine. It's a mess, though," she warned him. "Between the renovations and the wedding, I'm going a little crazy. There are artificial flowers and baking experiments everywhere."

Brad rubbed his hands together with glee. "I love experiments. At least we won't be hungry while we're writing the speech."

She threw her head back and laughed, feeling some of the tension from the parking lot melt away. This was the Brad she remembered—the friendly big brother with an enormous appetite and an endless source of laughs. "We just ate dinner! How can you still be hungry?"

He patted his flat stomach and gave a smug smile. "I'm a growing boy. I need food."

Brook elbowed him in the ribs, then stepped forward to unlock the door. She glanced around the apartment as she stepped inside, trying to see it from a man's perspective. This was the first time she'd brought a man into her apartment, and she'd gone on a *lot* of dates since buying the building. But she wasn't dating Brad, she reminded herself again. No reason to be nervous.

She hung up her coat and gestured for Brad to do the same. She'd never paid much attention to the entranceway, but now she smiled at the pictures sitting on a side table. The largest picture was one of her with Avery and her grandfather at their high school graduation. She'd been friends with the Brown family for a long time.

Brad turned to shut the door. He jumped as the door flew out of his hands. "Sorry about that. The wind's picking up. I hope the storm doesn't change their wedding plans."

As he walked into the apartment, Brook pulled a bowl of dough out of her oven. "This storm makes me nervous. Let me move this bread, and then we can work on the speech."

Brad stared at her as she washed her hands, greased a pair of bread pans, and slid dough from a bowl into the pans. "The bakery's closed tomorrow. What are you doing?" He hesitated, then moved toward the sink to wash his own hands. "Do you need help?"

He stood behind Brook, waiting for the right moment to reach the faucet. He still bumped into her in the small kitchen.

"Sorry about that." Brook stepped aside to avoid a second collision. "No help necessary. I wanted some fresh bread to make sandwiches for tomorrow. Just a little snack while we get ready."

She covered the bread pans with clean dish towels to finish rising, feeling a sense of satisfaction that she'd be able to feed her friends tomorrow. Baking was a joy for her, and her favorite way of showing that she cared. Brook was blessed to have a job that she loved.

Brook had mixed and kneaded the dough before the rehearsal. For once, she hadn't used the bread to purge her feelings. It was a nice change from a few weeks ago, when she'd made bread just to punch something. She'd been in a much better mood since she started working with Brad. *Not something Brad needs to know*, she thought.

She turned to ask Brad if he'd rather work at the kitchen table or the living room, then stopped. Brad had taken off his coat to reveal jeans and a form-fitting shirt underneath. He'd changed clothes after the rehearsal dinner. She took a moment to admire the muscles under his shirt and mentally shook her head. She wasn't going there. She wouldn't mess up the awkward friendship they were slowly rebuilding.

Brook cleared her throat and sent the speech she'd prepared on her phone to a nearby printer. "Pick a seat. I'll show you what I've written, and we'll make the speech work for both of us."

"We should tag-team each other and have fun," he said. "We've both known Grant and Avery for most of our lives."

"You're Avery's big brother. You've known her since she was born," Brook said dryly.

"Good point. Do I make a joke about seeing her in diapers? Nah, that's not right. Maybe we should make a joke about *us* dating. The two of us didn't work out, but we're happy our friends did."

Brook gaped at him. "It was one date! We don't have to tell the whole town."

Brad chuckled and leaned back in his chair. "I'd agree with you, but the town already knows."

She stared at him with wide eyes. What did he mean? No one had seen them together, and they'd avoided each other for years. "Explain."

"Avery's already warned me not to hurt you. She asked me to stay away from you." He winched. "I'm not sure if Grant knows. He's oblivious to these things, but I think he'd be rooting for us. I'd get another lecture first, though."

Of course Avery knew. She was one of Brook's most perceptive friends. She'd had to notice that Brad stopped coming home when she was baking at their house. He'd avoided the bakery once it opened, too. A lot of small things had changed once he started avoiding her.

Still, tomorrow wasn't about their past. It was about Avery and Grant, and their new life together. "I don't care who knows. We can't make the speech about us! Besides, there is no 'us.' Not now. Not ever." Brook was overcome with a sense of sadness. "Not ever" sounded an awful lot like "forever." Forever was a long time to avoid someone. "I know this is hard. I can give my generic maid of honor speech, and you can stand next to me and look pretty in your pink shirt. Avery won't hold it against you."

Brad waved away her concerns and grabbed the pen out of her hands. "Let's just focus. I can say that I lost touch with Grant after high school, but I'm thrilled to have him back in our lives. I couldn't be happier for them." His words sounded happy, but he scowled as he spoke. Brad tossed the pen down in frustration and rubbed his face with calloused hands. "I'm happy for them. I really am. But I wasn't here for this. I came in at the end, the big brother who couldn't save our grandfather's house. I moved in after Avery and Grant had fixed everything."

Brook leaned forward and put a hand on his knee. She could almost feel the guilt radiating off him. Brook understood how he felt. She'd been in Sunset Cove the entire time, watching Avery work herself to exhaustion while she tried to earn money to pay for the overdue taxes on her home. Sure, Brook had given Avery a job—but her friend wouldn't accept any other help.

To her surprise, Brad gripped her hand tightly. He all but growled as frustration filled his face. "I wasn't here when my sister needed me. That still haunts me. I'm trying to do better, though."

Brook squeezed his hand back. "You're doing great. The last time I saw Sophia, she couldn't stop talking about Uncle Brad. I'm not sure if she's more excited to have an uncle in town, or a new dad. She's lucky. Not every girl has two good men in her life."

"I'm glad that I'm here to watch Sophia grow up. I've got a lot to make up for." He cocked his head toward Brook. "Thanks for being there for my family. You were Avery's first friend when we moved to Sunset Cove. You supported her when she came home last year, too. Now I'm here to support you. Return the favor, if I can. Obviously, I'm all-in for your bakery renovations, but if you need anything else, just ask."

Brook blushed and stared at the floor. She hadn't seen this side of Brad before. Sure, he was a good brother. But he'd never gone too far out of his way to help other people. She cleared her throat, then shook her head. "I'm doing okay on my own, but thanks. I'll let you know if I need anything."

Feeling uncomfortable, she looked around for a distraction. Her eyes landed on a tray of muffins. "Let's finish up this speech. I've still got to bake bread, and we'll both be up early tomorrow." She leaned over to grab the muffins and held them out, hoping he would take the bait and stop reminiscing about the past. "Here's a snack to help."

Brad's face lit up with a grin. He grabbed two muffins off the tray and peeled off the first wrapper. He moaned quietly. "Triple chocolate muffins. I remember these from college." He took a bite and closed his eyes, nodding. "There's something different about them. They're even better now."

She snorted. "It's the taste of experience. There's a splash of espresso powder in this batch. It kicks up the chocolate flavor, doesn't it?"

He nodded in agreement and stuffed the rest of the muffin into his mouth. "Okay, let's keep working on this speech. I'm thrilled for Avery and Grant and happy to wear pink on their special day. What else?"

Brook smiled as she picked up the pen and began jotting down notes. Her newest muffins had Brad's approval, and her best friends were getting married tomorrow. Life was good.

Chapter Fifteen

Brad

―ele―

Sunset County EMS

Remain on alert for an evacuation order.

Be prepared to leave with a week's supply of clothes and medication. We continue to monitor conditions.

Brad looked up from his phone and frowned. This wasn't what Avery and Grant needed on their wedding day.

As the only man in the bridal party, Brad would get to the church later than the bridesmaids. The girls were already there to have their hair and makeup done. He would run errands and do anything else that the bride asked.

Brad finished buttoning up his dress shirt, tugged on a water-proof jacket, and made sure his tux was sealed in its garment bag. Then he rushed to his truck in the pouring rain, sliding a bit on the slick sidewalks. The cold front was moving in, bringing icy surfaces and lots of wind with it. Today's weather would be nasty.

I've got a few minutes. Let's check the waves, he thought, heading in the opposite direction of the church. He drove the short distance to the ocean and stopped to stare at the water. The wind was whipping the waves higher than normal, nearly reaching the boardwalk. He prayed the waves wouldn't come any higher. It would take a miracle to stop a flood at this point.

He turned the truck around and headed toward the church. Brad parked as close as possible and dashed inside with his tux. He rushed inside, almost flattening the florist standing by the door. "Sorry! Trying to get out of the rain. Can I help you with those flowers?"

She nodded and gestured to the pen and clipboard on top of a large box. "If you wouldn't mind, I need someone to sign for these flowers. I'd find the bride, but I'm in a bit of a hurry today."

Brad picked up the pen and signed for the delivery, then slid the box out of her hands. "No problem. I'm the bride's brother. I'll get these to the right people."

"Thanks, I appreciate it." The florist sighed and looked out the window. The rain was turning into big, wet snowflakes. "This is my last delivery. I'm not waiting for an evacuation order—I can't risk being stranded here with my elderly parents. We've got a hotel room reserved an hour inland."

Brad nodded. "I understand. Drive carefully, and thank you for the beautiful flowers." He watched out the window as she dashed to her car and sighed. He couldn't blame her for leaving town. Would anyone stay for the wedding?

He walked to the choir room and knocked on the door. The bridal party had taken over the room, turning it into a dressing and prep area. "Is everyone decent? It's your favorite bridesman. I've got flowers!"

He heard giggling and women shuffling around in high heels. A moment later, Brook opened the door.

"We're all dressed. Come in," she said, holding the door open.

Brad didn't say anything. He didn't step across the doorway, either. Instead, he drank in the beautiful woman in front of him.

Brook was a lovely woman on an average day, but the dress and makeup had transformed her. Today, she looked incredible.

"If you don't stop staring, I'm going to get uncomfortable," she announced. "You're being weird."

Brad cleared his throat. "Sorry about that. You're beautiful. I mean, you're always beautiful," he stammered. "But you're extra pretty today."

"Of course I am. We're here to support Avery, and we want to look our best. But look at your sister! She's the beautiful one today."

Brad tore his eyes away from Brook. His sister stood in the corner, looking nervous. She bit her lip and gave him a small smile. "Is it too much? I'm not one to get dressed up."

Brad's heart warmed as he walked up to Avery. He held out his arms and gave her a gentle hug. "You look phenomenal. Grant is one lucky man."

As he pulled back and watched the bridesmaids and little Sophia fuss over Avery's dress, he considered what made Avery look so special today. Sure, the dress was beautiful. Her hair was nice, too. But more importantly, she radiated happiness. It was like someone had tucked a ray of sunshine inside her soul, filling the room with brightness and joy.

Grant had done that. Brad felt a sudden pang of jealousy. How did it feel to know that you'd made someone incredibly happy?

He watched as Brook straightened Avery's veil. When Brook glanced over and caught him staring again, he didn't drop his gaze. For a moment, he imagined Brook was the woman in white, beaming with joy. The thought gave him a small thrill.

Stop it, he warned himself. Brook didn't want a relationship. They were friends. Besides, this was Avery's day. He needed to get his act together and focus on his sister.

When the girls had finished fussing with Avery's dress, Brad opened the box of flowers. He pretended to take a big sniff, then handed the largest bouquet to his sister. It was filled with soft pink roses and peonies. "Beautiful flowers, for a beautiful bride," he added.

The next four bouquets were identical. He hesitated for a moment, then handed the first flowers to Rachel. Emma and Kerry came next. He saved the last bouquet for Brook, accidentally-on-purpose letting his hand skim over the maid of honor's arm as he handed the flowers to her.

Brad was rewarded with a tingle that ran up his arm and seemed to shoot straight into his brain. The girl was getting to him.

He cleared his throat and handed his niece the smallest bouquet. Brad held up the box and the men's boutonnieres. "Where are the groomsmen hiding?"

"They should be here in thirty minutes. The men got ready at home," Brook said. "You should finish getting ready, too."

He nodded and shrugged on his tuxedo jacket, then folded and tucked his pink handkerchief into the pocket. "Done!"

The energy in the room continued to rise as they waited for the wedding to start. Brad sent up another prayer that the day would go smoothly, and that the weather would cooperate enough to give Avery and Grant a beautiful day.

Sunset Cove's residents were made of tough stuff. They wouldn't let a snowstorm stop them from seeing the town's newest couple tie the knot.

Avery's phone chirped just thirty minutes before the wedding would start. She reached for her purse and frowned. "I hope that's Grant. He should be here by now."

There was a knock. A muffled voice came through the door. "It's Pastor Rick. Can I come in? This is important."

Brad groaned. This was a bad sign. The pastor wasn't supposed to stop by until it was time to leave the choir room. He opened the door to see a frazzled-looking pastor standing in the hallway.

"Ladies, Brad. I hate to do this. Grab your bags. We've got to leave."

Avery gasped and rushed toward the door. The joy she'd spread throughout the room had disappeared, replaced with confusion and a darker mood. "Tell me we're not using the backup plan. Not now."

Brook whirled around and stared at her best friend. "What backup plan? What's going on?"

Brad took a deep breath and gathered the flowers from each bridesmaid. He packed each one back into the florist's box.

When he came to Brook, she pulled her bouquet out of his reach. "No way. Tell me what's happening. Why are we packing up the flowers?"

He glanced up at the pastor. "I'm guessing the mayor's evacuating Sunset Cove. The waves were close to breaching the boardwalk this morning. If this wind drives the waves any higher, the roads will flood at high tide."

Pastor Rick nodded. "You should get a text from the town's alert system soon. The mayor called me first, because he knew so many people were gathered at the church."

Sophia looked up at her mom. "Are we going to drown?"

"Of course not, sweetie." Avery crouched in front of her daughter with a sad smile on her face. "We're moving the wedding to a better place. Somewhere not so close to the ocean."

The girl's lip quivered. "I don't want to leave. Our car could float away."

Brad crouched next to his sister and niece. He took Sophia's hand. "If it was too dangerous to leave, I would tell everyone to stay here. But it's better to go now. Think of it as an adventure!

We'll go to another church for the wedding. We'll all eat together and have a sleepover."

Sophia wiped away her tears with an impatient brush of her hand. "I've never had a sleepover. Are they fun?"

"Sleepovers are the best," he promised. "Why don't you help your mom pack up, and I'll ask Pastor Rick how I can help everyone get to the new church in time for the wedding."

He stepped out into the hallway and started to close the door behind him. Before the door was halfway shut, Brook barreled out of the room. She poked him in the chest and glared at him. "Why are you telling Sophia that we're moving to a new church? What are you doing?"

Brad held his hands up in defense. "It wasn't my idea. Avery and Grant wanted a backup plan. They knew an evacuation was possible, and needed to give their guests a safe place to go."

Pastor Rick stepped between the two of them. "I've got a friend whose congregation will unlock their doors and turn on the lights. That's all we need. Besides, the people of Sunset Cove need somewhere warm and safe to stay. What better way to keep them calm than to throw a wedding?"

Brook's jaw dropped. She glared at Brad. "You're serious?"

"Unfortunately."

"This is crazy! We should postpone the wedding until after the storm passes. No one will mind."

But Brad laughed and moved toward the choir room door. "I think Avery will mind. Grant, too. The poor guy waited almost ten years to marry my sister. He told me at the rehearsal that a little snow couldn't stop him."

Brook huffed and stared at the ceiling for a few moments, then looked back at Brad. "You're impossible. Okay, if this is happening, we need to move. Let's load everything into Grant's truck."

"Grant left the church a few minutes ago." Pastor Rick grimaced. "He wanted to drive Avery and Sophia himself, but I encouraged him to help with the evacuation. I promised to get the bridal party out safely. He wasn't happy about it, but each of the men took their truck. They're helping the people who can't drive."

The door to the choir room opened, and the rest of the bridesmaids marched into the hallway with garment bags and the box of bouquets. They'd already changed out of their dresses and into everyday clothing.

Brook sighed. "Let's grab the cake. I've still got the boxes I transported it in, so it should be fine in my car."

Brad put out his arm to stop her. "No, not your car. It's too small. It's not safe to drive it in this storm."

He looked at the rest of the bridal party and remembered Grant's request—to keep Brook safe and make sure she left town. "We'll pack everything in my truck. I've got the extended cab for supplies, plus I can fit one person in the front seat. Brook can ride with me. Does anyone else have four-wheel drive?"

Rachel raised her hand. "My SUV does. I grew up in Michigan. I can handle the snow and ice. If you're willing to take Brook and the supplies, I can take the rest of the people."

Brad nodded, switching into autopilot. "Let's do this. The storm will only get worse if we wait. Where are we going?"

Avery pulled up a map on her phone and showed it to Brad and Rachel. "It's about an hour northwest of here. It's well outside of the evacuation zone. We should be safe from the worst of the flooding."

"I need to stop at the bakery," Brook announced. "Finish packing up. I'll be back in a minute."

Brad groaned. Grant had been right; Brook had no sense of self-preservation. Her first concern was always the bakery. He grabbed her arm. "What do you need? Everything you need should be here."

"I need to make sure the shop is locked and ready for the storm," she argued. "I'll drive back to the church and leave with you. I promise."

Brad felt a familiar unease stirring in his gut again. "Be quick. We'll pack the truck."

He pulled his waterproof coat over his tuxedo jacket, then helped the rest of the bridal party grab their bags. They filled the back seat of his truck with the dresses and flowers while Avery packed up the cake, tucking it carefully into Rachel's trunk. He gave his sister a hug and pushed her into the SUV. "You've got a storm to outrun. Get going."

"Please be careful," she replied. "I need you and Brook there on my wedding day."

He nodded and slammed the car door. It wasn't until his sister and her friends had driven away that he realized Brook still wasn't back. She'd been gone over thirty minutes.

The bakery was only a few minutes away. What was taking her so long?

Fueled by nerves and angry that he'd let her take this risk, Brad climbed into his truck and headed toward the bakery.

Chapter Sixteen

Brook

Brook dashed around the bakery, grabbing bags of flour and sugar from the bottom cabinets. She rushed to put each bag on a higher shelf.

She still believed what she'd told Emma while they made centerpieces. Flooding wasn't likely. Still, the price of raw ingredients was insane. Brook couldn't afford to replace everything if the bakery flooded.

Like most business owners along the coast, she had flood insurance on the building. It would cover any flood damage, but only after she paid a hefty deductible. It wasn't something she wanted to consider, especially since she planned to remodel the bakery after the storm.

Brook was deeply focused on her task when the back door to the kitchen flew open. She let out a shriek, then calmed down when she saw Brad standing in the doorway. An angry, wet Brad. His jacket dripped with snow as he rushed into the room.

"What are you doing?" he hollered. "I waited at the church, and you didn't come. We've got to leave."

Brook didn't pause in her work. She grabbed an enormous box of custom napkins, menus, and other paper goods and heaved it onto the counter. "Give me five minutes. If you want to leave sooner, help me."

Brad groaned, but he pushed the door shut against the heavy wind and moved to her side. "What are we doing? What's so important that you're risking your life and your best friend's wedding? You don't need to move things around inside the bakery."

Brook's face flushed with anger. "I'm not risking anything, and I'm not hurting anyone. I can't afford to lose this stuff if we take on water. Move these cupcake liners onto that shelf. I'll grab the takeout containers from under the cash register. I need to move everything higher."

She rushed around the storefront, muttering as she grabbed what she could. Brook prayed the waves would stop rising before they damaged the businesses closest to the boardwalk. The next few days would be stressful.

Together, Brook and Brad rushed around the bakery and moved the last of the paper goods out of cabinets and lower shelves. Brad straightened and took a quick spin around the kitchen. "The pans and trays will be fine. Should we turn off the power supply, or do you have pumps in case the water comes in?"

Brook gulped. She hadn't thought about the electricity. Turning off the power was on the town's evacuation checklist. Maybe it was good Brad had come looking for her. "No pumps. Just floor drains. The electrical box is in the storage room."

He rushed to the storage room, and Brook heard the *click*, *click*, *click* as he turned off each circuit breaker. The lights in the kitchen turned off, leaving only gray daylight to illuminate the room. She pulled out her phone and turned on its flashlight.

Brad emerged from the storage room, wearing a grim expression. "Power's off. There's nothing else you can do."

Brook nodded and sighed. Brad was right—they'd done all they could to prepare for the storm. Maybe Pastor Rick was right, too. They could still celebrate Grant and Avery's new life together while they put the town into God's hands.

Brad picked up her purse and tossed it to her, then held open the back door. "Let's go. We've still got to move your car to the church parking lot, where it's less likely to get damaged."

Brook pulled the door firmly behind her. She turned her back on the wind as she locked up the bakery, fiddling with the lock. The door had given her trouble lately. She'd add a doorknob to the list of things she needed Brad to replace once they came back.

She struggled to walk through snow and slush that was nearly as high as her boots, toward the car and truck that were barely visible through the snow. Nor'easters sure could drop a lot of snow. It was time to leave.

Chapter Seventeen

Brad

BRAD CLUTCHED THE STEERING wheel of his truck as he watched Brook's car slip and slide up the hill to Grace Lutheran church. What had she been thinking?

He knew she'd put a lot of money into the bakery, but no amount of money was worth staying in town. Besides, they were almost an hour behind the rest of the wedding party. People would worry, and they'd hold everyone up.

Brad gave a sigh of relief when they pulled into the church parking lot. She parked her car and dashed toward his truck, nearly slipping in the slush. He shook his head. This woman was driving him crazy. He'd promised to keep her safe, and she made that job very difficult.

She hopped into the truck and slammed the door, pulling the big, wet snowflakes inside with her. Despite his anger, Brad couldn't help but notice how beautiful she looked with glittery snow in her hair. He reached over to brush off the snow, then hesitated.

"What's wrong?" she asked.

He closed the gap between them and gently brushed the melting snow out of her hair. "It's just snow, but your hair will be all wet when it melts."

Brad pulled his hand back and drummed on the steering wheel. "Put your seatbelt on. Let's get out of here." He paused until he heard her seatbelt click into the place, then threw the truck back into four-wheel drive and slowly made his way down the hill toward town.

It was like driving through a ghost town. There were no people. No cars. There weren't even plows at this point. Only rows of empty, dark streets and houses.

Brook let out a sound of disbelief. "Everyone's gone. The mayor must have called for a full evacuation. I didn't even listen to the announcement. I thought the pastor was being cautious. We haven't evacuated the town since we were in middle school."

Brad gritted his teeth as he slid through a stop sign. He wasn't sure why he'd bothered trying to stop. There wasn't a single car on the street or side of the road. The cars that hadn't been driven out of town were parked on higher ground.

He thought back to the last time Sunset Cove was evacuated. While his friends had left reluctantly, confident that their parents were overreacting, teenage Brad had been numb with fear. His parents had died in a car crash on a snowy day. He knew how quickly life could turn from a pretty snowstorm, or a little flooding, into disaster.

Brook touched his arm and looked at him with concern. "Are you okay?"

"I'll be fine. The GPS says we're only forty-five minutes away. We'll be there in no time."

"All we've got to do is unpack everything and set up the wedding. Piece of cake." Brook gasped. "Tell me the wedding cake is in the truck."

Brad shook his head again. This woman needed to get her priorities in order. "I carried it from the church kitchen to Rachel's vehicle. We needed Avery's help to get it in the box, though."

He'd urged them to leave everything behind, but Rachel had been adamant about bringing the cake. It was Brook's gift to Avery and Grant. So the bakery box had gone into the SUV, surrounded by bags and luggage to keep it from sliding around.

Brad thought this announcement would make Brook happy. Instead, she buried her face in her hands.

"The cake was a surprise! I can't believe Avery had to pack up her own wedding cake."

"To be fair, Avery was the only one qualified to do it. If I'd helped, it would have fallen on the table. Or the ground."

Brook raised her head out of her hands and glared at him. "That's supposed to make me feel better? Give me a moment to grieve. I was looking forward to Avery's reaction. I worked on the design for *weeks*."

Another wave of guilt washed over Brad. If he'd known how important revealing the cake was to Brook, he could have taken pictures. Avery had looked delighted, though. Lots of gushing, and she even shed a tear or two. He told Brook this. "And at least we'll have dessert tonight. The caterer isn't part of the backup plan, but there will be cake.

She sighed and sat back in your seat. "You're right. They've had to move their wedding to an evacuation shelter, and I'm worried about the cake. We've got bigger problems."

The two of them drove in silence. Brook fiddled with her phone, trying to find information about the flooding. After a few minutes, she pointed to the dashboard. "Can we turn the radio on? I could use some music. They might have some storm updates, too. I'm not getting any service on my cell phone."

Brad nodded. He tried not to breathe too deeply as she leaned over to reach the radio, but couldn't help but notice her perfume. She smelled like vanilla and honeysuckle again, nearly good enough to eat.

He held back a chuckle. He didn't think Brook would appreciate his thoughts, even if she worked in a bakery.

Brook searched until she found a station that serviced southern New Jersey. She leaned back in the seat and gave a little shimmy as music filled the truck. "That's better. It was too quiet in here."

Her respite from worrying didn't last long. As the song ended, the blare of an emergency warning signal sounded from the radio.

We have an important storm update. Authorities have issued a mandatory evacuation for Sunset County, including the borough of Sunset Cove. Conditions are rapidly deteriorating and there is a high probability of flooding throughout the area. The National Weather Service has issued a warning for localized storm surges within the next forty-eight hours.

Stay tuned to WKJE as we keep you updated on this week's storm.

Brook grabbed Brad's arm and stared at him with wide eyes. "A storm surge? That's not possible."

Brad glanced down at her, then focused his attention back on the road. "It isn't likely, but nothing's impossible. We can't do anything now, though. We've got to keep moving forward and get to the church. It'll be safer once we're off the roads."

He silently reached out and turned off the radio. The announcement had chilled him to the bone. He never thought he'd see a storm surge in Sunset Cove. The last surge had happened almost forty years ago, according to his grandfather. Flooding was one thing. But watching the ocean rise to meet you? It was a terrifying thought.

Equally terrifying, he knew there was nothing he could do. He couldn't protect Brook's bakery, or anything else in town. Like the ice and snowy roads that had caused his parents' accident, the ocean had a mind of its own.

His only option was to get Brook safely to their evacuation point.

His knuckles were nearly white from gripping the steering wheel when he finally pulled into the crowded parking lot of Midtown Lutheran Church. As he turned off the truck and turned to face Brook, his phone rang. It was his sister calling.

"Is everything okay? The whole town's here, but I can't find you. Everyone says they haven't seen you yet."

Brad unbuckled his seatbelt and tried to reassure his sister. "We just got here. My truck's parked outside the church. We need help unloading this stuff."

Avery let out a shaky breath. "I was worried you hadn't made it out of town in time. Even the road crew evacuated to Midtown, so I knew the plows weren't running anymore."

"Sorry about that. We lost cell service along the way."

"It's fine. I was worried, though. We'll be outside in a few minutes to help unload the truck. We're coming out the back door. Meet us there?"

Brad pulled his truck up to the door, where Grant and the rest of the groomsmen waited. It wasn't snowing nearly as hard in Midtown. They'd left the worst of the storm behind them. It was still remarkably windy, though.

"Long time, no see," Grant said, grinning at his friends as they started pulling garment bags out of the truck.

Brook stared at him. "You're cheerful. It's not like our entire town is flooding. Or that your wedding day is ruined."

Grant continued to smile. "Nothing's ruined. We're all here, and we're safe. I'm still going to marry my best friend. It's the best day ever. Not even a storm can bring me down."

As they emptied Brad's truck, he asked Grant what time the wedding would start. Clearly they weren't following the set schedule—by this time, the happy couple should have been in the reception hall, cutting cake.

"Pastor Rick says there's no rush. We've got nowhere to go, so we'll start the wedding when everyone is ready."

Brad shook his head as he tucked his phone into his pocket and zipped up his coat. "Grab your stuff, Brook. We've got a wedding to start."

Chapter Eighteen

Brook

Brook looked around in amazement at the fellowship hall of Midtown Lutheran Church.

They'd decorated the hall back home. She felt a wave of sadness as she thought about the beautiful flowers, ribbons, and centerpieces they'd left behind.

Midtown's church had something that they didn't have back home—it was filled with people they loved. They were here to wait out the storm, but also excited to help Avery and Grant start their new life together.

Sophia whirled around her in excitement. "Aunt Brook! Aunt Brook! It was a beautiful wedding, wasn't it?" The six-year-old gave a sigh worthy of a made-for-television romance. "I love a good wedding."

Brook choked back a laugh. That girl was full of spunk. She'd started calling her Aunt Brook a few weeks ago. It was an honorary title, but Brook hadn't stopped her. She loved the kid as much as she'd love any niece or nephew. Besides, Brook was an only child. This was her only chance to claim the title of "aunt."

Brook gave the girl's braids a gentle tug, then held out her hand to spin the girl in circles. It *had* been a beautiful wedding. It was a shame about the storm, but the people were what made it beautiful.

Sophia spun faster and faster, chattering as she went. "It was really nice, and I heard there's going to be music soon. Can you dance with me?"

"Oh, honey. I don't think we're having music. Even if the DJ evacuated with us, I doubt he brought his equipment."

Brad tapped her on the shoulder. He gave her a wide grin when she turned around. "Sophia's right. The DJ had his equipment in his van. When the evacuation order came through and he heard Pastor Rick's plan, he started driving."

She shook her head in amazement. This must be the most exciting evacuation Sunset Cove had ever seen. "I left my speech at the church, though. It was in the worship hall. I forgot to grab it."

"It's okay. I have a copy." Brad grinned as he pulled out his phone. "I took a picture in case I wanted to practice."

This man thought of everything, she thought in amazement.

"Let us know when you're ready. The DJ wants to announce us first, like a normal reception. We'll dance for a bit before the speech."

When the wedding party gathered outside the hall, Brook stood near the back.

Brad held out his arm and led her to the front of the group. "We're going in first, remember? The maid of honor and the bridesman walk together."

Brook blushed, feeling the warmth of his arm through his tux. They'd skipped walking down the aisle after the wedding, since they'd filled the center and side aisles with chairs for the overflow of people. Instead, they'd simply walked out to the side annex.

It had been a simplified wedding, but beautiful. Grant's face had glowed when he saw Avery for the first time. She'd hidden her dress from him during the chaos once they all arrived in Midtown. At least they'd managed one surprise.

Brook grinned as the DJ announced their names and the rest of the wedding party, then watched as the bride and groom danced together for the first time.

The second dance was the bride and her brother. Brook held back tears as she watched Brad with Avery. It wasn't fair that their parents and grandfather couldn't be here.

Grant walked over to join her as the siblings danced. "Avery looks happy."

That was it. She really was going to cry. Brook wiped away a few tears as she turned to Grant and nodded. "I'm glad she's happy. You both deserved a great day."

"In a funny way, today was even better than I imagined," he replied. "In what world would I gather the entire town for a wedding? I've got so many friends in Sunset Cove. We never could have invited them all. But look." He gestured to the crowd of people. "Everyone that I love is here."

Brook stood in silence, absorbing what Grant had said. Her friend always had a positive attitude. He could take the worst situations and find a reason to smile.

As the song ended, Grant reached up to straighten his tie. "It's our turn to dance again. Maybe you can find happiness tonight, too."

Brook watched him in confusion as he walked away and smoothly twirled Avery in a circle. As the next song started, she heard the DJ announce that this dance was for the bridal party. She'd forgotten that would happen. She looked around and realized her friends were already on the dance floor—each in the arms of a groomsman.

Brad stepped into her line of sight. He held out his hand and smiled. "May I have this dance? I think they're expecting us."

He glided her into the middle of the group, moving with the beat while he smiled down at Brook.

She looked up at him, wondering where Brad had learned to dance. "If I didn't know any better, I'd think you were enjoying yourself."

Brad's eyebrows shot up in surprise. "Of course I am. I'm dancing with a beautiful woman. I'm happy for Avery, too. I wish she hadn't gotten married in the middle of a storm, but she doesn't mind. That's what matters."

Brad and Brook gently swayed to the music, their eyes locked on each other. Brook was overcome with the emotion and romance of the day. There was something about weddings that made you believe in love.

I wonder what it's like to love someone like Brad, she thought. *He's turned into a great guy.* She opened her mouth, then hesitated. What could she even say?

Brook's thoughts were interrupted by the DJ's booming voice. "Okay everybody, let's gather together," he announced. "It's time for the toast and the maid of honor's speech. The bride's brother will join her."

Brook swallowed the lump in her throat. Did the DJ have to interrupt them now? She'd been having a moment with Brad. But maybe this was better—her "moments" with guys always ended in disaster. Especially moments with Brad.

She pasted on a smile and accepted the microphone, then walked to the front of the crowd with Brad. Time to focus. They'd settled on a speech filled with humor, and hopefully, love. "We've both known Avery and Grant for a long time."

"I've known Avery since the day she was born," Brad quipped, leaning in to make his joke. The wedding guests chuckled, just as they'd hoped.

Brook took the microphone away from Brad, her smile warming as she began their story. "I've known Avery since she moved to Sunset Cove in elementary school, and I met Grant when we started kindergarten together. He always shared his crayons with me." The crowd murmured "awww," encouraging her to go on. "Being best friends is not the same as being siblings, but it's pretty close. I was an only child, but I never felt lonely after Avery moved here. She was my best friend and honorary sister. I even had an honorary big brother." She turned to Brad and gave him a genuine smile as she handed over the microphone.

"I watched Avery grow up overnight," Brad continued. "We'd just lost our parents. That does something to a kid. But she was welcomed warmly in Sunset Cove, and quickly became friends with Brook here—and Grant. I watched Avery and Grant together for *years*. They claimed to never be more than friends… Sometimes I had my doubts." This time, he joined in as people laughed. "Now that they finally admit they love each other, I couldn't be happier for them. I'm proud to be part of their special day. See, Avery, I even wore pink for you!"

Brook grabbed back the microphone, like they'd planned. "It was Brad's idea to wear pink." The crowd laughed even harder. Brad shrugged and smiled. "But like Brad said, we've watched Avery and Grant's friendship grow over the years. We're both thrilled to be part of today, and can't wait to see what comes next in their journey together."

Brook attempted to juggle the microphone while she opened a water bottle, making a loud scraping noise and nearly pouring water on the floor. Brad gave a nervous chuckle and reached out to open the bottle for her. She nodded her thanks, then spoke again. "I know this wedding wasn't what they'd planned. We don't have fancy glasses or bottles of champagne. But let's raise our drinks in a toast." She raised her bottle of spring water. "To Avery and Grant. May they have a lifetime of happiness together!"

The crowd murmured in response, raising their water bottles, cans of soda, and even a few cups of coffee in a toast.

Brad patted her on the back as they walked away from the crowd. "We did good with the speech, especially since we only had an hour to write it."

Brook laughed. "It was perfectly acceptable. We made them laugh, and I even saw a few people cry. It was quality work."

Brad turned to her and raised his red plastic cup in a second toast. "Cheers to supporting the happy couple, and to working together. We couldn't have pulled off this wedding without you."

"Here's to us," she agreed, taking another sip of warm water. Brook stared up into his eyes, worried again that she might say something stupid if she didn't get her act together. She wasn't in love with Brad. That would be ridiculous. She was getting swept up in the romance of the past few hours.

So instead of saying something she might regret, she smiled. "I wish every wedding was like this. It was cozy and a little chaotic, but it was perfect and…" Her voice faltered as the hall's lights flickered out. She stood in the darkness, listening to Brad's breathing as her eyes strained to adjust to the dim light from the windows.

Grant was the first person to break the silence. "I've got a generator in my truck! We'll get the lights back on."

Cozy and chaotic, indeed.

Chapter Nineteen

Brad

MARRYING THE OWNER OF a construction company wasn't the worst thing his sister could have done.

Grant hadn't even prepared for the backup plan. He had a generator in his work truck when they'd evacuated. His crew never knew when they'd need a power supply.

Brad shook his head in amazement as he looked around the church hall. He'd helped Grant and Nick drag the heavy cord from the generator to the power box in the church. In just a few minutes, they had enough electricity for the lights and DJ's speakers.

Once the lights were back on, the party continued for hours. Brook and a few other creative souls even put together a decent meal with donations from Midtown's congregation.

Brad leaned against a wall and bit into his sandwich. The music was slowing down. He glanced over at the kitchen, where Brook juggled stacks of plates and plastic forks. That could only mean one thing—it was time to cut the cake.

His hunch soon proved right. The DJ faded out the music and grabbed the microphone. "Let's turn our focus to the front of the room! Our bride and groom are going to cut the cake in a few minutes."

Avery and Grant cut the first slice of cake, illuminated by dozens of camera flashes. They worked together to slide the chocolate cake onto a paper plate. They'd picked out a cake cutter and special plate for the occasion, but neither had made the journey to Midtown. The couple didn't seem to mind, though. Avery beamed at her husband as he popped a small bite into her mouth, then turned to offer Sophia a bite, too. The little girl cheered when the sweet treat hit her taste buds.

Brook pushed a food cart filled with cake slices around the room. "Want a piece?" she asked Brad. "My over-planning turned out to be a good thing." She looked around the crowded room. "I thought we'd have lots of leftovers. Instead, we'll have almost enough for everyone."

"Thanks. I've been looking forward to cake all day. It's a shame there won't be leftovers." He eagerly took the plate and moaned as he ate the first bite. Brook had found her calling when she opened the bakery.

Emma walked over to the cart and nudged Brook into an empty chair. "Time to sit. You've been on your feet all day, making food and feeding people. Let me pass out the cake. Here, have a slice." She handed Brook a piece of cake, gave her a stern look, and began walking away. "Take a break!" she yelled over her shoulder.

Brook sighed as she sat back in the chair, perching the plate of cake on her lap. "I'm a little tired," she admitted. She scooped up a bite of cake and scrutinized it, then placed it in her mouth. Brook closed her eyes as she considered the flavors. "I'm glad I used fondant. Buttercream wouldn't have survived the drive."

Brad poked at the icing and shrugged. "Is this what fondant is? It's tasty. Whatever it is, I'm glad Grant didn't smash the cake into Avery's face. It's done in good fun, but I wouldn't enjoy having cake smashed in my face."

"What wedding are you planning?" Brook smirked. "Give me a few weeks' notice. I'd be happy to make a cake for you and your bride."

Brad coughed, nearly choking on a bite of cake. "What are you talking about? I'm not getting married!"

"Since when are you so easy to rile up?" Brook laughed as she gave him a few hearty thumps on the back. "I teased you constantly in high school, and you never took the bait."

Brad cleared his throat and took a long drink of bottled water. "You caught me by surprise. Thanks, but no. I won't need a wedding cake anytime soon. I don't have women pounding on my door."

"That's too bad," Brook said. She shook her head and chuckled darkly. "If it makes you feel better, women who spend their life inside a bakery aren't in high demand, either. I work too much. Every guy says so. When I'm not working, I'm too tired to have any fun."

"I think you're lots of fun. Clearly, you've been dating fools. Any man would be lucky to spend their lives with you." Brad reached out with a napkin, then hesitated. "You've got a bit of icing, right here." He handed her the napkin and gestured to his cheek.

"Thanks." She wiped her face clean and tossed the napkin in a nearby trash can. "I'm glad you liked the fondant. The store-bought stuff tastes horrible, but it's pretty good if you make it from scratch. The secret is to add vanilla bean paste."

Brad nodded and took another bite of cake, feeling awkward now. How could he possibly add to the conversation? What Brook did in the kitchen was a little like magic. Everything about her, from her smell to the way she smiled, seemed magical.

He was just the fool who had broken her heart.

The two of them stood in silence for a few minutes. Brad continued to search for something to say. All he could think was, "You look beautiful" and "This cake is great." He kept both thoughts to himself.

Brook finished her own food and hummed happily. "I hope Avery liked the cake, even if it wasn't the surprise I'd planned. I outdid myself this time. The strawberries and chocolate were a perfect mix."

Brad stared at the floor and mentally smacked himself in the head. Of course he should have talked cake with Brook. They were supposed to be friends, and cake was her entire world. When would he stop being so nervous around her? He'd been fine dancing with her. Dancing at a wedding was normal. Natural.

Being stranded in a church hall, with nothing to talk about? Not natural.

Brook clearly didn't have the same level of awkwardness. She scraped a stray piece of icing off her plate and tossed both of their plates into the trash. "Thanks for the company. I should see if Emma needs help." She dashed into the kitchen to wash her hands, then began searching for her friend.

Brook was one of the kindest people he'd ever met. Any man would be lucky to have her in their life.

He'd been lucky enough to date her, so he should know. He just hadn't been smart enough to stay.

Brad really was a fool.

Pastor Rick tapped the microphone, making it squeal from feedback. Brad flinched. What a way to end the night.

But Pastor Rick was still in high spirits. He grinned as he clutched the microphone. "Sorry about that! The lights are turning off in forty minutes. We'll have one last dance, and then everyone should find a cot or blanket and a comfortable place to sleep. We're safe tonight, and we've got a lot to be grateful for. Let's be patient and all get some rest."

He handed the microphone back to the DJ, who nodded and played a slow, moody song over the speakers.

Brad stood near the wall. The rest of the wedding party gathered for the last dance. He wasn't sure where Brook was, but they hadn't danced since the beginning of the reception. He'd sit this one out. Brook wouldn't mind.

He was surprised by a tap on his shoulder. Brook stood with her hand on her hips, her eyebrows raised. "You weren't avoiding me, were you?"

"Of course not. I thought you'd have your feet up. It was a stressful day for all of us."

"And miss the last dance? No way. Come on, they're waiting for us." She pointed to Avery and Grant, and all of their friends, who were waving them toward the group. "One more dance, and then you can go back to avoiding me. Until you remodel my kitchen, of course."

"I wasn't..." he objected.

Brook laughed and held out her hand. "I'm sorry, I shouldn't tease you. But seriously, we should get out there."

Brad let himself be pulled to the center of the room. His heart thumped faster as he thought about dancing with Brook again. Getting close enough to smell her intoxicating scent. Wrapping his arms around her...

Okay, so he was still attracted to her. It was time that he admitted it to himself. There was nothing he could do about it, though. Tonight should be about Avery and Grant. This wasn't the right place to confess his feelings. So he kept his mouth closed before he could say anything he'd regret, and smoothly guided her through the dance.

While Brad was a fool, he wasn't foolish enough to turn down this dance.

As the song ended, Brad slowed to a stop and smiled at Brook. "That was fun."

"It was. We should do it again sometime." She gave his hand a quick squeeze, then dropped her arm. "I'm going to help hand out blankets. Can I sit with you after the lights go out? I'm not up for a girl's night." She looked over at Emma, Rachel and Kerry, who were laughing with Avery's and Emma's daughters as they prepared for bed. "Not that you're second place or anything. You're just... calmer. I need calm tonight."

Brad blinked twice, trying to clear his head. Sit with Brook in the dark? That sounded like a bad idea. For what felt like the hundredth time, he reminded himself that they were only friends. No other feelings allowed tonight. So instead of arguing that they should sleep with the rest of the wedding party, he followed Brook toward Pastor Rick, who was handing out blankets.

Brad was soon in charge of moving the cots. There weren't nearly enough beds for the entire town. They were saving them for the elderly and handicapped, who would have the most trouble sleeping on the floor.

Brad followed Harry Anderson with one of the last beds, holding a loud conversation with his grandfather's old friend.

"I was hoping we could go home tonight. It sounds like the water hasn't reached its peak though, so it's good we're all here," Harry yelled over the voices echoing through the hall. "No serious damage yet. But I don't know if the worst is over. I've seen a few floods in my day, and they can hit hard after your guard is down."

Brad's gut twisted as he considered Harry's words. He was glad there hadn't been too much damage—yet. It would be stressful waiting for news as the water continued to rise.

He set up the man's cot and added a blanket. "It's not much, Harry. But this should get you through the night."

The old man winked. "I've slept on worse. At least there are some pretty women here to keep us company."

Brad smiled. "Can I get you anything before the lights turn out?"

"This will be just fine. You looked good dancing with Brook. Grab yourself a corner with her. Make sure you snuggle real close."

"I'm not sure what Brook would think about that." Brad laughed as he walked away. Harry was a lot of fun to be around, but his thoughts on women usually made him shake his head.

By the time he returned to Pastor Rick, the pile of blankets was nearly gone. Brook was nowhere to be seen.

"Only take what you need," the pastor said as people grabbed supplies. "We're all friends here! Don't be afraid to share."

Brad hesitated, his hand hovering over the pile of blankets. How many did he need? And more importantly, how angry would Brook be if he asked them to share a blanket? He sighed and picked up a wider afghan for them both to use. Brook wouldn't want anyone to go cold.

"Have you seen Brook?" he asked the pastor.

"She's in the kitchen, putting the last of the food on ice. We can't leave the generator running overnight." Pastor Rick glanced around the hall, which was already growing chilly without the church's heating system. Even if they could use the generator all night, it couldn't run the heat. "I wish we had more blankets. It's going to be a long, cold night."

Brad helped Brook move the last of the sandwich fixings into coolers. He stepped back to look at his friend. She'd changed out of her bridesmaid dress and into a sweatshirt and jeans, plus a thin winter coat, but she was still shivering. Chilling the leftovers hadn't helped her stay warm.

He set the blanket aside and pulled off his tuxedo coat, then wrapped it around Brook's shoulders. He zipped up his own winter jacket and held out the blanket, a sheepish look on his face. "There aren't enough blankets. We'll have to share. But at least we'll be warmer if we sit together."

Brook pulled his coat around herself and nodded, trying to stop her teeth from chattering. "Whatever works. Sorry, I'm a wuss in the cold."

They found a relatively empty corner of the room to share. Brad fluffed his duffle bag the best that he could, trying to make a pillow for the two of them. He laid down with the bag under his head and patted the hard floor, then covered himself with half of the blanket and waited for Brook to join him.

"How should I..." Brook paused awkwardly and kneeled on the floor, staring at the space next to Brad. She laid down with her head on the bag. She twisted and turned until they laid back-to-back under the blanket.

Brad listened as her breathing slowed, and her body relaxed. The last thing he heard before he drifted off to sleep was, "Thanks, Brad. You're nice and warm."

Chapter Twenty

Brook

Brook slowly opened her eyes. There were hundreds of people in this room. Where was she?

Oh, it doesn't matter, she thought. *It's so warm under this blanket.*

She snuggled closer to the person next to her and closed her eyes again.

Her eyes stayed shut, but that didn't stop more questions from popping into her head. Who was she sleeping next to? And why was this bed so hard? It was like she was sleeping on a concrete floor...

As Brook's brain slowly engaged, she realized what had happened. They were in a shelter. The town had evacuated after flooding threatened Sunset Cove. She was lying on the floor. Next to Brad. Cuddled up as if they spent every night together.

She gave a small squeak and shifted carefully, holding her breath as she untangled their legs and shifted away from Brad.

Brook didn't relax until she was standing next to Brad, looking down at his still-sleeping figure. At least he was a heavy sleeper. It was awkward enough waking up next to him. She needed to freshen up and find coffee before they spoke again. She shrugged off his coat and draped it over him, then tiptoed away.

Dim light filtered through the nearby windows, and she could faintly see her breath when she exhaled. That meant the power was still out. Grant had mentioned that they were running out of gas for the generator. Besides, the generator only powered the lights, not the heating system. They might face another chilly night and more shared blankets. The thought both thrilled and embarrassed her.

As she walked to the bathroom and waited in line, Brook knew she was being silly. She should be grateful they had somewhere to wait out the storm. The members of Midtown Lutheran Church had donated food and blankets, too. Even if she had to share blankets and huddle up with friends to stay warm, it was better than being stranded in a flooded apartment.

But if she was home, she'd know what was happening with the bakery. Not knowing was frustrating. The water levels would likely peak at high tide this morning. All they could do was wait for the water to recede.

Brook walked out of the bathroom a few minutes later. Washing her face and brushing her hair had perked her up considerably, even if they didn't have hot water.

Next, she looked down at her rumbling stomach. Time to figure out breakfast. At least she could put her cooking and baking skills to use.

They'd need to get creative with breakfast. The church had an older gas stove. She knew how to start them without electricity, and she'd be able to heat any food they scrounged up.

Pastor Rick was already busy in the kitchen, pulling boxes of cereal out of an enormous cardboard box. "We've got instant coffee if you need it. The Midtown grocery store dropped off some food this morning. Cereal, milk, bowls and plastic spoons, too. They said there was also... Ha! Found it." He opened the second box and started stacking loaves of bread on the kitchen island. "Twenty loaves of bread, and ten dozen eggs. It will be easier than working with five loaves of bread and two fish."

"I'm good, but I can't work miracles," Brook agreed. She mixed herself some coffee, then rummaged through the church's pantry and pulled out salt, sugar, and vanilla extract. "Thank goodness they use this kitchen regularly. I'll make French toast casserole for a few hundred people. For the rest, we've got cereal."

When Pastor Rick nodded his approval, she got to work chopping loaves of bread into cubes and preheating the oven. Brook had just started making syrup when Brad stumbled into the kitchen.

"Coffee?" he mumbled. "Please tell me there's coffee."

"There's instant coffee, and hot water on the stove," she said, pointing toward the gas stovetop.

Brad stirred sugar and coffee into his cup, then took a deep breath over the hot drink. "Thanks. It's not as good as the bakery's stuff, but I'll take it. How can I help you?"

Brook looked up in surprise. Sure, Brad had helped her pack the food away last night. But he worked in construction. She hadn't expected him to help with the meals. "Can you stir a pot?"

"I can make spaghetti. Does that mean I'm qualified?"

She laughed, feeling the rest of last night's awkwardness fade away. "You're qualified. This is simple syrup with a dash of vanilla. There's no maple syrup for the French toast, but this should work. You stir it until the sugar dissolves, and make sure it doesn't boil over."

Brad drained the rest of his coffee and gave her a mock salute. "Will do, boss."

They worked together while Pastor Rick bustled in the background, making more coffee and offering cereal to those who didn't want to wait for a hot meal.

This is cozy, Brook thought. It was nice having company while she whisked together eggs, milk and vanilla, then poured the mixture over her bread cubes. She shook her head, unsure where that thought had come from.

It didn't take long for her to prep the second and third casserole trays. She sprinkled some cinnamon sugar on top and slid them into the oven. "How's the syrup coming?"

Brad looked up from the pot, continuing to stir with his brow furrowed. "It smells good. And I can't see the sugar anymore. Does that mean it worked?"

She laughed and took the spoon from him. She gave the syrup a quick stir. It was starting to thicken. "Great job. Thanks for getting this done." She reached out to turn off the gas to the stovetop, and nodded. "We'll let this cool while the casserole bakes. More coffee?"

He walked to the counter that separated the main kitchen and hall, and grabbed two more cups of coffee from Pastor Rick. He nodded his thanks and grabbed a few packets of sugar for each of them. They both sweetened their drinks in silence. When they were done, Brad held up his cup in a toast. "Cheers. Here's to the bride and groom, and to keeping the residents of Sunset Cove safe, happy, and well-fed."

"I'd toast to that, but I've had three cups of coffee already," Pastor Rick shouted over his shoulder.

Brook laughed and raised her cup before taking another long sip. She wrinkled her nose. "I'll toast to that too, but I'm looking forward to a good cup of coffee."

"Soon," he promised. "The worst of the storm should be over today. We've just got to wait for them to lift the evacuation order. Then you can go back to making coffee, and muffins, and cookies..."

Brook smacked his arm. "Stop it. You're making me hungry."

Brad patted his stomach. "I'm hungry too! I'm a grown man who has needs, and those needs include muffins. Could you make a few in this old stove?"

She shook her head. "There aren't any trays, or wrappers. Or butter. We've got to make do with what we have."

"Well, I'll be first in line when Seaside Cupcakes reopens."

The two friends grinned at each other. It would be nice to get back to normal. Things had been anything but normal over the past twenty-four hours.

Brook's smile slid off her face as she thought about all that had happened yesterday. Asking Brad to dance, sharing a blanket, and waking up snuggled next to him. "About last night…"

But Brad waved her concerns away. "It's fine. We're friends, right? Friends can keep each other company when they're stranded in a strange place. We'll go home soon, and this will all be a memory."

As he said this, a humming noise filled the kitchen. Brook glanced around in concern. Her heart gave a jump of joy when she realized it was the hum of the refrigerator. The power was back on.

Grant walked into the kitchen with a grin on his face. "Good morning! I disconnected the generator last night, so this is straight from the power company. One problem solved."

Grant looked between his two friends, trying to read their moods. He walked to the counter and picked up two cups of coffee. "I'll grab some caffeine for my bride and get out of your way. Find me if you need anything!" He walked away, humming.

As he left, Brad turned to Brook and gave a wry smile. "That's one of your problems solved. We'll have heat tonight. No more sharing blankets."

Brook nodded, surprised to realize that the thought made her sad. As awkward as it was to wake up next to Brad, it was the best she'd slept in years. She rarely slept with men—most men didn't make it past a second date. Brad was good company, even when they were sleeping. He made her feel safe.

But only because they were friends.

· ♥ · ♥ · ♥ · ♥ · ♥ ·

Brook spent the next two days in the Midtown kitchen with Avery. Together, they made soup, sandwiches, and enormous trays of pasta for their friends and neighbors. Keeping these people fed was a full-time job. Brook didn't mind staying busy—it kept her mind off the flooding in Sunset Cove.

News had spread through the hall like wildfire. There was significant damage to a small part of the town. A few of the businesses near the boardwalk had been hit hard.

Since no one was allowed back into town yet, they made do with rumors and news on the radio. Brook didn't know if Seaside Cupcakes was damaged. She just kept cooking. The hours of chopping, stirring, and serving felt like a constant prayer. *Let my bakery be okay. Give me a business to come home to.*

Brad and Grant alternated their time between the kitchen and a makeshift office in the church's meeting room. The employees of Grant Construction were preparing themselves for the return to town. They'd have a lot of work ahead of them. Pastor Rick joined them a few times to discuss how the Kindness Committee could help.

The sleeping arrangements in the large hall were less awkward now. More blankets had been donated. The room wasn't nearly as cold when the electricity and heating system worked. Brook and Brad slept with the rest of the wedding party, separated by their friends and a foot or more of floor space.

If Brook was honest with herself, she might admit that she missed Brad's company. Instead, she told herself that it was for the best. Brad would be fine without her. And she didn't need a man to keep her happy or warm.

She did need to serve lunch, though. It seemed like mealtimes came faster, with shorter breaks, each day.

"Soup's ready," Brook yelled, pushing a cart filled with bowls of chicken noodle soup. It was amazing what you could make with some creativity. A few cans of vegetables, lots of noodles, and canned chicken could make a hearty meal.

Brook sent up a prayer of thanks for the donations they'd received. She was also grateful for her years of catering experience. She hadn't cooked meals for a crowd in years, but it was like riding a bike. The skills had come back quickly.

Harry Anderson was the first in line. He rushed to the food cart and took a bowl of soup. "Ms. Brook, you are an angel living on earth. This soup smells heavenly. I don't know what we'd do without you."

Pastor Rick patted Harry on the back, agreeing. "We're fortunate to have her here."

Brook blushed as she helped Avery pass bowls of soup to hungry hands. "It's nothing more than what I do every day," she assured him. "It's not my usual cupcakes and cookies, but I love filling bellies and raising people's spirits."

After helping to feed the first wave of people, Pastor Rick accepted a bowl for himself. He lifted the spoon to his mouth and sipped the broth, then smiled. "You've done a great job. If you expanded your bakery to include food like this, I'd be the first person in line."

Brook's eyebrows rose. "People would buy this? Soups, sandwiches, things like that?"

Avery nodded, gesturing toward the tables of people. "They've gotten a sample of what we can do with donations. Imagine what kind of food we could make with more planning. Besides, it's the perfect time to consider expanding the menu."

Brook paused as she reached for another bowl of soup, then put her hands on her hips. "Avery Brown, are you saying we should expand the bakery even more? Add a lunchtime menu and prep area while everything is ripped apart?"

"Yes! That's exactly what I'm saying. We should do it. What do you think, Pastor Rick?"

"I think it's a great idea. May I have another bowl of soup?"

Brook returned to portioning out the food, her mood notably brighter. At least one positive thing had come from the evacuation—she had new inspiration for her business.

Chapter Twenty-One

Brad

Brad and Grant stood in the kitchen, stirring the deep pots of soup that Brook and Avery served out in the hall. The women would be back for refills soon. For now, the two men were alone.

It was hard work feeding the people who had evacuated to Midtown. Brad knew it wasn't too different from Brook's job. Sunset Cove welcomed thousands of people during tourist season, and Seaside Cupcakes was the most popular bakery in town.

On top of that, Brook did everything with a smile. Brad worked long hours in construction, too, but he spent that time with the crew, or alone with his tools. After three days in Midtown, Brad had discovered that he was *not* a people person.

All he wanted was to go home. He itched to pick up a hammer and start rebuilding Sunset Cove. But more than anything, he wanted to be at Seaside Cupcakes, helping Brook make her bakery even better than it was before.

He might not be a people person, but he craved a few hours of Brook's company. Minus a few hundred other people.

The urge surprised him. He'd dated lots of women. None of them had grabbed his attention like Brook Reed, and he wasn't even dating her.

Brad stirred the chicken soup with more vigor than necessary, making the soup slosh onto the counter. He grabbed a fistful of napkins to clean up the mess, then turned to Grant. Maybe a conversation with his friend could distract him. "I guess this isn't how you imagined your honeymoon."

Grant laughed and shook his head. "We were planning to wait until Easter break. Just a quick trip while Sophia's off from school. That won't happen now. We both agreed that the town needs us." Grant grabbed a rag and helped Brad clean up the rest of his mess. "I didn't imagine spending my wedding night with hundreds of people. It's fine, though. No one will forget this wedding. What about your girl? How's Brook holding up?"

Brad stood up, nearly bumping the pot of soup and making an even bigger mess. "My girl? I'm not dating Brook."

"*Can you hold me? It's cold in here,*" Grant teased in a falsetto voice. "You looked cozy that first night. Nothing like sharing a blanket to start a relationship."

"It's not like that." Brad held his hands up in defense, trying to reassure Grant. "We're just friends. We had a thing as teenagers, but that's ancient history. Brook doesn't want to date anyone right now."

Grant leaned against the counter and crossed his arms. "Brook's a great girl. You'd be foolish not to jump at this chance. Just don't forget that she's my friend. She's your sister's best friend, too. Don't hurt her."

Brad nodded, then picked up the soup ladle and stirred again. He'd expected the warning from Grant. "She's amazing, right? I messed up with her a long time ago, and Brook doesn't give second chances."

Grant shrugged and picked up their second crock pot. He placed it next to the stove and began filling it. "I messed up with Avery, too. It turned out okay. We just needed to trust each other again."

"How do I do that?"

"Be her friend. Show that you've changed. And then you both decide if you want more than friendship."

Brad nodded, searching the crowded hall for Brook. "I'll take this soup out to her. Brook could use more help. She's been working too hard."

"That's the spirit," Grant said. He patted his friend on the back, then held the kitchen door open as Brad wheeled the soup out on a cart. "Send Avery back to the kitchen, won't you?"

Brad nodded to people as they shifted out of his way, making a path to the tables where Brook and Avery served food. "Are you ready for a refill?"

Brook turned to him and smiled. "Thanks. We're almost out of soup. Let me empty this pot, and you can swap out the carts."

"Grant wants to see Avery in the kitchen. Maybe she can take it back. I'm happy to help you, though."

Brook finished ladling out the contents of the first pot and shrugged. "I could use the help. Avery needs a break, anyway."

As he watched his sister walk away with the first cart, Brad frowned at Brook. "When will *you* take a break? You've been on your feet since dawn, too."

"I don't mind. Avery's juggling a lot. She's a mom, and now a wife. I'll take my break when she comes back."

Brad let out a sigh of impatience and snagged a nearby chair. He dragged it toward the food cart and pointed at it. "Sit. Eat. It's break time." He handed Brook the bowl she'd filled with soup, then slid a spoon into the bowl. "You can't put everyone else's needs first. Take care of yourself, too. I can handle the food for a few minutes."

She sat back with a huff and ate a few bites of food. Then Brook ate faster, like she'd just realized it had been hours since her last meal. Brad guessed that she'd skipped breakfast and went straight into lunch preparation.

When she finished eating, she sighed and looked up at Brad. "I'm sorry. I'm exhausted, and I don't know how much longer I can keep this up. Thanks for making me take a few minutes." She frowned as she stared into the empty bowl. "I'm not sure if I've eaten today. Everything is blurring together."

He shook his head and handed her a bottle of water. "You probably aren't drinking enough, either. I've got this."

Brad stood at the food cart, ladling out bowls of soup, while Brook rested. The line never seemed to end. He shook his head, feeling angry at the town's residents. Didn't they see how hard Brook worked? He was grateful his sister had Grant. Someone needed to look after Brook, too.

He placed himself squarely in front of the food cart, nudging Brook aside when she tried to help. Brad pointed to the chair again. "Ten more minutes. Stay off your feet for ten more minutes."

When her break was over, Brook and Brad worked together to keep feeding the town. They made a good team; Brook filled the bowls as quickly as she could, and Brad handed bowls and utensils to the people waiting. He noticed that the line moved faster when they worked together.

Grant came out twice to swap out their empty pot for a full one. Avery was also resting, Brad noticed. That was good.

As the last people sat down to eat, Pastor Rick approached Brad and Brook. "I'll make an announcement in a few minutes, but I'm talking to Kindness Committee members first," he said, keeping his voice low. "The mayor is reopening Sunset Cove tomorrow morning. We can go home."

Brook's attention snapped toward the pastor, all signs of tiredness gone. "What does the town look like? Did he give you any updates?"

He nodded, his face settling into a frown. "The mayor drove around with the National Guard today. Main Street looks okay, but the houses and businesses closest to the beach all have some damage. We won't know how bad it is until we get inside the buildings."

"Did he mention the bakery?" Brook asked. "How far did the water go?"

The pastor placed his hand on Brook's shoulder. "I don't have a lot of details. Main Street is three blocks from the beach, and we know the water didn't reach Main Street. Your bakery is a lot closer to the ocean. Let's just pray that none of the damage is serious. We've got some hard workers in our town, and we'll work together to make everyone whole."

Brad reached out to put his arm around Brook, then hesitated. He'd been fine calling Brook a friend—until Grant put the idea of dating back into his head. Was it okay to hug a friend? He wasn't sure.

Still, he didn't want to pull away from her again. Brad gently wrapped her in a hug. "We'll fix any damage and finish remodeling the bakery. Get you back on track."

Pastor Rick nodded. "That's right, young man. I hope to see you at more Kindness Committee meetings. We're going to need you, and all of your friends, when we get home tomorrow."

Brook sighed as he walked away. "I'm glad we can go home soon. I'm scared to think about what I'll find, though."

Brad put his hands on Brook's shoulders and spun her toward him. "You're not alone in this. You've got Grant, Avery, and me. Sunset Cove is my home now. I want to help you."

Brook brushed away a stray tear and smiled. She leaned closer, wrapping her arms around him in another hug. "Thanks, Brad. I'm glad we're friends again."

Friends, he thought wryly, resisting the temptation to lean in and smell her hair. Even with their strange living arrangements, she still reminded him of vanilla and fresh bread. It would be tough to stay friends and ignore his feelings for Brook. *Thanks, Grant.*

Brook didn't have that problem. She continued working, making sure no one at the tables needed more food and cleaning up the unused bowls. When she was done, she sat down to eat a second bowl of soup. Brad wheeled the food cart back into the kitchen.

He found Grant and Avery scrubbing out empty pots. Grant turned to face Brad and gestured toward the hall. "Well? How did it go? I tell Avery everything, so don't hold back."

Brad rolled his eyes. "It was awkward. Thanks for that, by the way. I just made peace with being her friend. Now I keep noticing how nice she smells."

Avery threw her head back and laughed. "It's like her pores absorbed the cupcake batter. I hope it happens to me, too."

Grant leaned in to sniff Avery's neck. "I like how you smell. Don't change it."

"Don't mind me. Keep smelling my sister. It's fine." Brad dropped the empty crock pot on the counter with a clatter.

Grant chuckled and turned his focus back to his friend. "Feeling awkward is the first step. It means you care. Time to get comfortable being uncomfortable."

Chapter Twenty-Two

Brook

Brook stared out the window of Brad's truck as they drove into Sunset Cove. As promised, the mayor had lifted the emergency evacuation order. The local National Guard's disaster response team had cleared the roads of debris. They could all head home—but what would they find?

"Oh, no. Not the school," she gasped as they drove past Sunset Cove Elementary. A large tree had fallen onto the building. The school groundskeepers were already there with chainsaws, trying to remove the tree. Branches had broken through the front foyer's roof and damaged the main entrance.

Brad's grip tightened on the steering wheel until his knuckles were white. "Grant Construction will be busy."

They drove slowly, taking care to avoid the occasional sand drifts that remained in the road.

Brook dropped her head into her hands and moaned. "Can we go straight to the bakery? I know you want to check on your sister's house, too. Just drop me off. You've got enough to worry about."

Brad reached out and rubbed her back in comforting circles. Friends or not, he wouldn't let her feel alone. "Grant texted me. Their house was built to survive this type of storm. They're fine. You will be, too."

Brook nodded and stared out the window. The bakery was less than a mile away. It seemed like the storm had hit some buildings hard, while sparing others. This part of town was far enough from the shore to avoid rising water—there were just lots of fallen trees and branches in yards, and the occasional broken window or roof damage.

Seaside Cupcakes was closer to the beach than the school and these houses, though. It was more vulnerable to the waves and sand.

She let out a shaky breath as the bakery came into view. It didn't look too bad. A tree in front of the bakery had blown over, but missed the building. She sent up a small prayer of thanks. Branches littered the front sidewalk. They could be cleaned up.

When Brad pulled his truck into a parking spot, she jumped out and shoved her key into the bakery's front door. The door opened easily. But something wasn't right.

Brook was used to walking into a clean, well-lit building filled with fresh bread and baked goods. The room was bright enough from the sun, illuminating a floor streaked with mud. And the smell... It made her stomach turn.

She stepped out onto the sidewalk again and turned to Brad. "Something's wrong. Why does it smell so bad?"

Brad pushed the door open, making the welcome bell jingle. He poked his head inside and stepped back out. "Mold."

"Mold, already? We were gone for three days!"

"It doesn't take long. We need to dry out the building. You should wait outside." He walked back to the truck and pulled out a pair of rubber boots. "Mold is nasty stuff."

Brook stood in front of the bakery door with her arms crossed. "It's my building. I'm going in."

Brad hung his head for a moment, then nodded. "I'd feel the same way. Don't tell Grant that I let you in the building, okay? And we're not staying long."

Together, the two of them walked into the customer's side of the bakery. Brad didn't seem concerned about the dirty floor. "The smell worries me. It might mean there's mold in these walls already. We might need to rip them out."

Brook whipped around to face Brad. What did he mean, rip the walls out? She'd only planned on a fresh coat of paint. She didn't have time or money to tear the building apart.

He pushed open the kitchen door, then let it fall shut again. Brad turned to face her. "Brook? Don't panic. It's a little worse in the kitchen."

She rushed toward the door. "Is that supposed to reassure me? Of course I'm going to panic now..." Her voice faded to nothing as she pushed through the door and stepped over the threshold, splashing into ankle-deep water. "No. This can't be happening. Why is the door open? And what is that SMELL?"

She recoiled as a stale ocean breeze hit her, mixed with the scent of mold. It reminded her of a musty, old fish shop.

The door to the alley hung open. That's where the breeze was coming from, she realized. Sand had drifted into a pile against the door, holding it open while the wind tried to push it closed.

Now that she looked closer, the kitchen wasn't just covered with water. There was a fine layer of sand and debris on the floor. From the looks of it, sand had clogged the floor drains.

Brad walked over to the door, rancid water sloshing over his waterproof boots. He jiggled the door handle. "Did this door give you trouble?"

"It was a little fussy. Sometimes it would stick, but I always used the deadbolt, so it didn't matter... We locked the deadbolt before we left, right?"

Brad jiggled the handle again. "I don't remember. We'll need to replace this lock, though. The latch is stuck." He used his boot to push some of the sand aside and close the door, then shook the handle one last time. It made a loud *click* as it popped into place in the doorframe. "The latch was already close to failing. It's just unfortunate that it happened during the storm."

Brook's temper flared as reality sunk in. "Unfortunate. That's an interesting choice of words." She sloshed over to the closet. The icy water wouldn't stop her from cleaning up her own building.

She yanked open the closed door and snatched a mop and bucket, then began the slow process of mopping up. Brook wrinkled her nose. The smell was awful. After a few minutes of effort, she paused. There was just so much water. She grew more angry, splashing water everywhere as she rang out the mop in frustration.

Brad looked up from the door, where he was busy taking the handle apart. He sloshed through the water and reached for the mop. "Let me help."

"I've got this," she snapped. "It's my fault the door was open."

Brad put his hand on her arm. "It's not your fault. I've got tools for this in Grant's office. You'll never clean this with a mop."

Brook yanked her arm out of his reach and plunged the mop back into the water. The past few days had been tough. She was tired, stressed, and overworked. It wasn't easy to take care of an entire town's food needs, even with help.

Now they were home, and she was facing the worst fears she'd imagined during the evacuation—flood damage in the bakery, and right before they'd started remodeling. She couldn't fix all of this on her own. That didn't mean she should beg for help every step of the way, though.

Besides, Brad was wrong. This mess *was* her fault. If only she'd checked that the door was locked! They'd still have to deal with flooding, but the sand was her fault. "Look, I'm grateful for your help. You got me out of town, and I couldn't have done that by myself. But I don't need someone to swoop in and save me. I'm used to working alone. It's fine."

Brook tightened her ponytail in frustration and pushed the bucket toward the door. She pushed the door open as the wheels hit the threshold. She tipped the bucket over. But instead of pouring the water outside, most of it splashed back into the flooded kitchen. "Argh!" she yelled. Her sneakers were already drenched, and now the icy water soaked her pants up to their knees.

Brad backed out of the room. Brook tried to ignore the look of hurt on his face, but knew she'd kicked him while he was down. All he wanted to do was help.

No regrets, she reminded herself. Brad had left her ten years ago, and he could walk out of her life again. She didn't care. She'd figure this out on her own.

To her surprise, Brad stopped at the edge of the kitchen. He still looked hurt, but a look of determination began to fill his face. "I need some tools, but I'll be back. You're not doing this alone."

Brook sighed and shook her head. "It's fine. You can leave." *You've always been good at leaving*, she thought.

"I'm not leaving. Like I said before, I'm going to help." He walked out of the kitchen and closed the door behind him. A few moments later, she heard his truck start and pull away from the bakery.

Brook felt her anger melt away once she was alone. Her whole life was a mess. Not just the bakery—her friendship with Brad was a mess, too. Why did she ruin everything she touched?

She hoped Brad would keep his word and come back. Despite what she'd said, she didn't know if she could do this on her own. Brook put down the mop and checked the cabinets. Everything in the lower storage units was wet. She'd moved all of her ingredients to the higher cabinets. They were still dry, but she couldn't tell if they'd gotten any moisture from the evaporating water.

Odor was another problem. How much had been absorbed by the flour? She couldn't risk baking cupcakes that smelled like rotten seaweed. She dragged her waterlogged shoes and clothing through the kitchen, then sat at the table next to her antique display case. Even the case hadn't escaped water damage. The wood was warped and swollen at the bottom.

Brook put her head on the table and cried. Everything in her life was falling apart. The bakery, her friendship with Brad, even her ridiculous display case that couldn't hold more than a few cakes and cupcakes. It felt like she was back in high school, listening to her parents argue and not being able to make it stop. Life would throw garbage at her, and she'd clean up the mess.

Why did she treat Brad so badly? None of this was his fault.

Guilt hit her as she thought about the day Avery had walked into her bakery last year. Her friend had needed a fresh start, and Brook had given that to her.

Brad deserved the same level of kindness. Instead, she'd rejected his help and pushed him out the door. She wouldn't blame him if he left again, for good this time.

This time, it would be all her fault.

Chapter Twenty-Three

Brad

Brad stomped into the office of Grant Construction and slammed the door behind him. He'd stayed calm with Brook, but couldn't help his temper now.

How many times must he tell Brook he wasn't leaving Sunset Cove? Brad was ready to stop running—from life, from relationships—but no one believed him.

Grant and Nick emerged from the office. Both had maps of the town in their hands. Nick's eyebrows rose when he saw Brad seething beside the front door. "Back so soon? I thought you'd help Brook clean up the bakery. How bad was it?"

Brad opened their supply closet and pulled out a shop vac and a box of trash bags. "I'm going back with supplies. She doesn't want my help, but she's getting it."

Nick hooted and leaned against the wall, crossing his arms. "This sounds like a good story. Let's hear it."

Brad's anger got the best of him. Words rushed out. "I saved her from a flooding town. I drove through a blizzard to get her to the evacuation site. After spending three days helping her cook and serve food, I brought her back into town and offered to help clean up the bakery." Brad paced back and forth in front of the shop vac, his voice rising along with his blood pressure. "Now she claims she's fine on her own, and she doesn't need me. But she needs my help. She doesn't realize how big of a job this is. And anyway, I *want* to help her." He ran his hands through his hair, tugging at the ends. "Is that weird? I don't want her to struggle alone through this."

"Given your history, it's a little weird," Nick said.

Grant sighed and pulled out the paperwork for Seaside Cupcake's renovations. "I care about you and Brook, but there's no time for games right now. Yes, you're going to help her. You're the foreman on this project. It's your job to rebuild the bakery." He flipped to the drawings that Brad had created before the storm. "If the foundation isn't damaged, we can fix almost anything. You'll continue taking point for this job. I can't afford to send any more men to the bakery. The rest of the town needs our help."

Brad nodded, hopeful now that Grant had his back. Brook would see reason. She had to let him help. "We'll need to gut the kitchen, and maybe the rest of the bakery. There's already mold in the walls."

Grant closed his eyes for a moment, the first sign that he mourned his friend's loss. This couldn't be easy for Grant. None of the town's damage would be easy for his kind-hearted boss. "Mold is bad news. What else can you tell me?"

Brad did his best to describe the damage in the kitchen, including the clogged floor drains and warped lower cabinets. He also told Grant about the faulty handle on the back door.

"That's an easy fix. Grab a spare handle out of the shed. We're always ready to switch out locks in case someone needs to secure a building." Grant looked over his notes, satisfied that he'd documented everything. "The water damage concerns me, though. We've got to get rid of the moisture as soon as possible. That means gutting the building, and fast. Can you handle that on your own?"

Brad threw up his arms in frustration. "I can handle the work if Brook lets me do my job."

Nick waved off Brad's concerns and ushered Brad into a chair. "We've been here before. Avery didn't want help, either. She insisted on handling her problems alone. She'd been hurt before, and had a hard time trusting people. Brook's been burned, too. Hasn't she?"

Brad gritted his teeth. "Sure, she's been burned. I was the guy holding the match. She's got no reason to trust me."

Nick grabbed a second chair and dragged it to the desk, deep in thought, as he examined his newest co-worker. "This could go one of two ways."

"Nick, don't mess with my crew," Grant warned. "We're here to get a job done. Everything else takes a back seat right now."

Nick held up his hands in surrender. "I'm not playing matchmaker. I'm helping Brad problem-solve the concerns of an unhappy client. We want Brook happy, right? And we need Brad in charge of the project."

Brad scowled as he shifted in his seat. "I want to help Brook. I wish I hadn't hurt her, but I'm ready to make it up to her."

Grant tossed the bakery's paperwork on his desk and crossed his arms. "Nick's a little unconventional, but his advice is generally good. He's the reason I've got a family now." Grant slapped Nick on the back. "But right now, Sunset Cove needs us to rebuild the town. I'm heading out to see who needs help. You two can talk for a bit, but then get to work. Got it? Take pictures for the insurance companies."

Brad watched his boss shrug on a coat and walk out the door. Grant was right. They needed to focus on rebuilding the town, not on his feelings for Brook.

Still, Grant had his happy ending. Didn't Brad deserve the same?

Brad wasn't a bad person. He was a person who'd made bad choices. There had to be a difference, and he would make better choices going forward. Deep in his heart, he knew rebuilding Brook's trust was his first step.

Nick continued to watch him. "Do Grant and Avery look happy?"

"Of course they do. My sister hasn't been this happy in years."

Nick grinned. "I did that. They don't call me the town matchmaker for nothing. Now that Grant's gone, are you ready to talk about your options?"

Brad cleared his throat and tugged at the collar of his sweatshirt. He hadn't realized there would be options. Nick should tell him what to do. "What options are there?"

"You could go to the bakery and help Brook. Get the building ready for a rebuild. When the project's over, you leave. You'll see her once in a while. Only when you're hungry for a Seaside cupcake, though."

Brad's stomach churned at the idea. Could he handle seeing her less often? Between the bakery and the storm, they'd spent a lot of time together. Was he ready for that to end? "Give me the second option. I like choices."

"First, I need to know your intentions with Brook."

Brad blinked, his thoughts fuzzy with confusion. "What intentions?"

"What are your plans? Do you want a one-night stand, or something more permanent? I know you're Avery's brother, but I'll always have Brook's back. I won't help you if Brook's going to end up hurt."

Brad nodded, impressed by Nick's comments. He could respect where Nick was coming from. After all, he'd hurt Brook pretty badly the first time around. He was glad Brook had people like Nick and Grant in her corner. Brad leaned forward, resting his elbows on his knees. "Can I be honest?"

"You'd better be honest. I've known Brook for a long time."

Brad cleared his throat and nodded. "I don't know my intentions. But walking away from her was a big mistake. She's an amazing woman. I should have treated her better when I had the chance."

Nick slapped his hand on the desk and stood up. "That's what I was hoping to hear." He walked over to the office mini-fridge and grabbed two waters, then offered one to Brad. "Like Grant said, I'm the relationship guy. I like figuring out why two people belong together, or what's holding them back. In your sister's case, she needed to know that Grant wasn't like her ex-husband. Avery needed time and space to see that Grant was different."

Nick paused for effect, twisting the cap off his water bottle and draining it. "So what does Brook want? What does she need to trust you again?"

Brad put his face into his hands, unease spreading through his body. He didn't like thinking about how he'd hurt Brook—and had no idea how to earn back her trust. Nothing he'd tried so far had worked. "I was hoping you could tell me. You're the relationship guy."

"Nope. You won't learn your lesson unless you figure it out on your own."

Brad growled in frustration. He finished his water and crushed the plastic flat. "I was an idiot, okay? I cared too much about her when we were kids, and that scared me. I ran away from my feelings. Does it make you happy if I say it out loud?"

Nick pursed his lips and shook his head. "I don't enjoy making people miserable. Let's dig deeper, though. Do you think Brook knew how much you cared about her?"

"I doubt it. I left town and avoided her for ten years." Brad's shoulders slumped. Talking about his behavior made him feel like garbage. He'd been a foolhardy teenager, sure. But even kids should know better. They shouldn't run away when they get scared. "I don't deserve a second chance with her, do I?"

"Probably not. But no one's perfect. All you can do is show Brook that you've changed, and hope for the best."

"How do I do that?"

"What did you do today? Walk me through what happened."

Brad had heard Nick liked talking about feelings and actions. Nick was the best at rebuilding friendships and bringing new couples together. He just hadn't realized how uncomfortable this would be. "I drove her to the bakery. We saw the damage. I tried to help her clean it up, but she told me to leave. She said she's 'used to working alone.'"

Nick shrugged his shoulders. "Do you know how much work it took to open that bakery? To keep it running? Most businesses fail within their first year. Seaside Cupcakes is growing, and Brook worked alone until she hired Avery last year. She's beaten a lot of odds, and she did it all without a man helping her. Keep that in mind."

Brad slumped down in his seat and frowned. "Thanks for the pep talk, Nick."

"No problem. I'm just reminding you that Brook is an independent woman, and she likes it that way." He paused again, considering what to say next. "I think she's lonely, though. She lives above the bakery and only goes on a few dates each year. Grant was one of her closest friends before Avery came back. They're still friends, but marriage changes things."

Brad felt his heart squeeze in sympathy. He understood what Nick was saying. Avery was his sister, but things were different now. Her new family was her top priority. Uncle Brad would always be there to support them, but Avery had a husband now—and Sophia had a new dad.

"You understand how Brook feels," Nick added. "You both seem lonely. Show Brook that you're not looking to take over her life. Support her. Encourage her. Just don't jump in like a hero and try to solve all her problems."

Brad nodded, letting Nick's words run through his brain again and again until they felt etched into his mind. "Support. Encourage. Don't be a hero. I can do that."

"Great. There's one problem, though."

"What's that?" Brad cocked his head in confusion, trying to figure out his latest misdeed.

"You left her again! You walked out and left Brook alone in a flooded bakery. That's not very supportive."

Brad threw his hands up in surrender. "I came here to get tools! I told her I'd be right back."

"Then go do that. Help her. Support her. Show her you're not leaving so easily."

Chapter Twenty-Four

Brook

Brook looked up as the bell over her bakery's front door rang out. Who could that be? She'd locked the front door after Brad left. Maybe there was a problem with that door, too.

With the luck she'd had, another broken lock wouldn't surprise her. Brook put down her mop and looked around the kitchen. She hadn't made much progress. With a sigh, she pushed through the watery mess and into the dining area. "Sorry, we're closed. We won't reopen until…"

She stopped talking when she saw Brad standing in the dark bakery. "Oh. It's you. I forgot you still had a key."

Brad slid the bakery key onto his keyring, but stayed near the door. "Sorry it took me so long. I got held up at the office. You didn't answer when I knocked. I hope it's okay that I let myself in."

Brook nodded, surprised that Brad had come back. She'd expected him to come up with an excuse to stay away. After all, she'd been adamant that she didn't need help. She had been wrong. "I'm sorry I told you to leave. Did you find a better way to clean up?"

He gestured toward the front window, toward the truck sitting outside.

She followed him outside and watched him drag a large, round vacuum into the bakery, then stood back and eyed the machine. "Can you use that in water?"

Brad nodded as he plugged in the shop vac and attached a long hose to the vacuum. "It'll suck up anything, wet or dry, plus it holds more water than your little mop bucket. Watch this."

Brook's eyes widened as he lowered the hose into the water. He began slurping up water more quickly than she'd imagined possible. In less than a minute, the vacuum bucket was full and the water inside the kitchen was slightly lower.

"It doesn't take a lot of water to make a big mess." He rolled the bucket outside, then poured the water into the grass. "You just needed better tools."

They worked side by side for an hour. Brad used the vacuum, and Brook went back to using a mop and bucket to soak up water. Once the water was gone, he spent some time trying to unclog the floor drain. The sand-filled drain would be more difficult to deal with, but Brad promised to find a solution.

When they'd finished, she turned to face her friend. "Thanks again. I'm stubborn and like to do things myself, but this would have taken forever. I appreciate your help."

Brad shrugged his shoulders and leaned against the kitchen counter. They'd propped open every door and window in the bakery, letting the icy ocean breeze usher out the scent of mildew and stale water. "I told you I'd be back. I wouldn't make you clean this up by yourself. We're still friends, right?"

She smiled widely and walked over to give him a hug. "Still friends." Brook let herself linger in his arms just a moment too long. Even in the musty building, he smelled so good. It had been a long time since she'd trusted someone enough to let him wrap his arms around her. If she wasn't careful...

Brook cleared her throat and pulled herself out of the hug. *Enough of that*, she told herself. Brad didn't do committed relationships. He might stay in Sunset Cove, but the last thing she needed was another whirlwind romance that ended in heartbreak. It was better if they just stayed friends.

Brad took a step backward and shoved his hands into his pockets. "I should get this vacuum into my truck. Grant wanted to canvas the town and find out who else needs help. Let me know if Pastor Rick calls you. I'm not on the Kindness Committee's phone chain yet, but I'm more than happy to help if he needs something."

Brook eyed the muscles under his long-sleeve shirt as he wrestled the vacuum out the bakery door. Clearly, he wasn't afraid of hard work. She shook the thought out of her head and rushed forward to help.

He loaded the shop vac into the truck, then turned to face Brook. "Give us a couple days to dry out the town, and then I'll get in touch. Keep your windows open. Turn some fans on. We'll do our best to keep your renovations on track. You've got a deadline, and only a small window between the holiday and the start of tourist season."

Brook groaned. "Valentine's Day! I had so many plans this year. What am I going to do?"

"Pastor Rick said you could use the church kitchen. It'll work out."

"Will tourists still come, after seeing the damage on TV?"

"The hotels are on Main Street, and the bed and breakfasts are further inland. They're fine. We might have some cancellations, but most people will be eager to see the town back on its feet."

Brook glanced down at the remnants of the tree in front of her store. There were small branches everywhere. She couldn't fix the mess inside her bakery without help, but she could start clearing the sidewalks. It would make it look like progress was happening.

She reached down to tug at the largest part of the tree trunk. It was blocking the sidewalk. It had to go, but it wouldn't budge. Brook pushed harder, feeling panic rise in her chest. She needed to be open for Valentine's Day. She needed that money to hold her over until spring. That was how beach towns worked. You stayed open year-round and hoped for local customers over the winter, but holidays like Christmas and Valentine's Day provided the boost that kept businesses alive until tourist season.

Brook took a deep breath and tried to stop her rising panic. Pastor Rick always told the congregation to count their blessings. No matter how bad things looked, you could find something positive.

At least the building wasn't a total loss. Brad said it could be fixed.

Another breath. The flood happened while they were remodeling, so they'd planned to replace and repaint a lot of things already.

Deep breath. Her insurance would cover some of the loss.

Three good things. That would have to be enough. She gave up moving the tree trunk and looked up at Brad, feeling hopelessness sink back into her soul. She wasn't sure if three good things could balance all the bad things.

Brad must have read the panic in her eyes, because he enveloped her in a hug. "It'll be okay. This is fixable." He rubbed her back in circles and pulled her close.

They stood huddled together on the sidewalk until Brad's phone went off. He pulled away and checked his messages. "I'm sorry. I would stay, but Grant's asking everyone to come back and regroup. He wants to focus on the heavy damage today. We've got a few homes with flooding, and the school groundskeepers need our help. But I won't forget about you." He paused, putting his hands on Brook's shoulders and looking her in the eyes. "I'll be back as soon as I can. Text if you need anything."

Brook nodded and watched him drive away. She'd told him she was doing just fine on her own. She didn't need a man to fix her problems. It was still nice to have someone like Brad on her side.

It was a shame they were just friends.

Chapter Twenty-Five

Brad

BRAD SPENT MOST OF the day driving around town, fielding requests from Grant and helping people pump water out of low-lying areas.

"You're a lifesaver," Harry Anderson said. "My back doesn't work like it used to." The elderly man had been lucky enough to avoid water damage in his home, but he'd had enough sand and branches littering his front steps and sidewalk that it wasn't safe to walk out the front door. Harry had been too stubborn to ask for help, but Pastor Rick had noticed the state of his sidewalks.

Brad nodded and shook the man's hand. "It's no problem. I'm glad Pastor Rick called us." He pulled out a business card from Grant Construction and scribbled his own phone number on the back. "Call if you need anything else. We're happy to help."

The man's eyes shone like he was holding back tears. "This means a lot. I know you're busy. Thanks for helping an old man."

Brad crossed his arms and narrowed his eyes at Harry. Why did everyone in this town hate asking for help? "You were one of my grandfather's best friends. Of course I'll find time for you! Keep that card. Call me. I mean it."

The old man chuckled and shook Brad's hand one last time, then used his cane to climb the steps into his house. Once Harry was inside, Brad got into his truck and texted Grant.

Grant was spearheading the recovery work from his own truck, keeping his team hopping from one location to the next. They'd done today's work at no charge. Brad was okay with that. Sunset Cove needed their help.

Harry's sidewalk had been an easy fix compared to the other problems they faced. Brad groaned when he saw Grant's next assignment—time to move fallen trees at the elementary school. Brad was dreading this job. He'd been too old for elementary school when they moved in with their grandfather, but he'd been inside the building when his sister was a student. The damaged front entrance would keep the school closed for a few days. Maybe weeks.

Logistically, opening the school was just the first step. Some families still hadn't returned to town, choosing to wait until the major cleanup and repairs were done. The houses on the outskirts of town still didn't have electricity.

He shifted his truck into drive and headed over to meet the rest of Grant's team. Workers had already cut the tree into manageable pieces. A dozen men loaded the pieces into trucks.

Grant pointed to the woodpile. "We're moving this to a field near the high school for the end-of-year bonfire. It only seems right that the kids should have some fun with the tree. It tried to tear down their school."

The two friends hauled logs and heaved them into the school's pickup truck. When they stopped to take a rest, Brad took off his gloves and grabbed a bottle of water. He handed a second bottle to Grant. "How's the rest of the town? Are we still getting requests for help?"

"We've cleaned up the worst of it," Grant replied. "I've got a few roofs to replace. A restaurant deck to rebuild. And Brook's bakery, of course. It could have been a lot worse."

Brad closed his eyes for a moment. He was grateful most of the town had been spared serious damage. Still, why did Brook have to lose so much? It wasn't fair. She'd worked hard to build her business, and now she was facing a complete rebuild.

"Brook was lucky," Grant said, seeming to read Brad's mind. "She had more damage than other shops in her neighborhood. But if this storm had hit in spring, she'd probably lose the bakery. We wouldn't have time to do repairs before tourist season. It's only February. We'll get her open before the spring rush."

Brad swallowed the lump in his throat. Even if they were only friends, he still cared about Brook. Fortunately, he could help her. He'd work as many hours as she needed to reopen. "I know it's a bigger project than we'd planned, but I'd like to stay in charge of Brook's bakery. Let the team focus on the rest of town. I'll focus on Brook."

"That's still the plan. I want Nick in charge of the smaller projects. He's got more experience juggling multiple sites and crew members. You work on the bakery."

After a quick conversation with the school groundskeepers, the two men headed back to their trucks. The bulk of the work at the school was done. It was time for both of them to get back to the bakery, to make sure Brad had everything he needed.

It didn't surprise Brad to see his sister's car in front of the bakery. What did surprise him was Grant's reaction. Grant jumped out of his truck, slammed the door, and stormed into Seaside Cupcakes.

Brad raised his eyebrows, then grabbed his clipboard from his truck dashboard and cautiously headed inside.

Grant and Avery stood toe to toe, arguing. Grant's face was red as he spoke. "There's mold. There could be asbestos. This is an older building. You don't know what you're breathing in. Take those gloves off and go home."

Avery stood her ground. She handed over the gloves and crossed her arms. "I'm not going home. I'll stay out of the kitchen, but I'm not leaving. Give me a job that I can do."

Brad watched them with wide eyes. He'd never seen them argue before, not once. But as he studied Grant's face, he realized his boss was more concerned than angry.

Sure, there was mold in the building. The short time they'd be here cleaning up and taking notes shouldn't hurt anyone. They had gear and masks to wear while they ripped out walls and floors. Why was Grant so worried?

Brook approached her friends with her hands held in a gesture of peace. "Is something wrong? I didn't mean to hurt anyone. If it's not safe here, we'll leave. Saving the bakery isn't worth making people sick."

Grant shook his head, but didn't break eye contact with Avery. His voice softened as he pointed toward the door. "Out you go," he said gently to his wife.

He turned to give Brook a small smile. "You can stay. Avery needs to leave, though."

Brook frowned. "I'm missing something. Avery, are you sick?"

Avery looked sheepishly at her husband, then turned back to her friends. "No, I'm not sick. Grant's being a little overprotective. I was waiting to tell people, but we could all use some good news. We're having a baby!"

Grant's expression softened as he looked at his wife. "Yes, we're having a baby. I couldn't be more excited. Now please get out of this building. I want a healthy baby and a healthy mom. You don't need to be breathing in this stuff."

Brad's jaw dropped. A baby, already? They'd just gotten married. Not that he was upset, of course. His niece was a great kid.

It didn't take Brook long to overcome her own shock. She clapped her hands in excitement. "A baby! I'm so happy for both of you. But Grant's right, you shouldn't be in here. Can we work outside the bakery? Avery can supervise me while I drag more of that tree away."

Grant hesitated, then nodded and pointed out the door. "Outside in the fresh air, please." He grabbed her hand and pulled her in for a soft kiss. "I love you. I'm sorry if I overreacted."

Brad felt a wave of disappointment as the women walked out the door. His sister's health was important, but Brad had hoped to spend the day with Brook.

Nick's words range clear in his head: support, encourage, don't be a hero. He mentally added, "Don't make a big deal when she walks away" to the list.

Being a good friend, and proving that you'd changed, was hard work.

Chapter Twenty-Six

Brook

Avery walked to the corner of the bakery's property and started to lift the largest branch blocking the sidewalk.

"What are you doing?" Brook asked. "You shouldn't be lifting anything heavy. You're having a baby!" She tugged the branch out of her friend's hand and squeezed her in a tight hug. "Congratulations, by the way. I'm so excited. Since Sophia calls me Aunt Brook, do I get to have another niece or nephew?"

Avery rested her head on her friend's shoulder and leaned into the hug. "You'll always be their honorary aunt. Sophia loves you like family, and I'm sure the new baby will, too."

Brook pulled back and looked at her friend. "How did Sophia take the news?"

"She's excited. Sophia begged Eric for years to give her a little brother or sister, but my ex-husband didn't even want his first kid. Not that he'd admit that to Sophia."

Brook shook her head and walked over to Brad's truck, where she pulled out a rake. "I'm glad Eric is out of the picture. He didn't deserve you, or Sophia. It's tough to find a good guy these days, but your ex-husband took the cake." She handed the rake to Avery. "I'd make you sit down and watch me work, but that would make you mad. Raking's okay, right? Just don't overdo it. We've got to keep my little niece or nephew safe."

Avery leaned on the rake and laughed. "Aren't you cute? I was rearranging furniture when I was pregnant with Sophia. I didn't know until three months along."

Brook tugged on a smaller branch. It wasn't too heavy. She could probably manage it herself, which was a good thing. It wasn't like she could ask Avery for help. As her boss, Brook would make sure Avery was on light duty for the rest of her pregnancy. "Don't push yourself too hard. How far along are you?"

Avery made short, efficient strokes with the rake, gathering twigs into a pile. "I'm guessing between four and eight weeks. We're thrilled, of course, but we weren't expecting to start a family so quickly." She laughed. "We wanted to try after the wedding. It's taken us too long to find each other. Besides, Sophia's almost eight years old. That's a big age gap."

Brook dragged the tree limb to the curb, next to Brad's truck. She was thrilled for her friends. Grant and Avery deserved some good fortune.

That happiness didn't stop a wave of jealousy from washing over Brook.

Didn't Brook deserve to find joy, too? She loved her business, but she woke up early to bake, then spent the day making her customers happy. When her workday ended, she climbed the steps to her apartment. Alone.

Being alone was all she knew. What if she could find someone to share a life with her?

Brook shook her head. That wasn't going to happen. Every man she'd dated had been a dud—either too immature to commit, or too selfish to imagine her as an equal partner in life.

Even Brad had fallen under the "immature" column. It was a pity they hadn't met later in life. She glanced through the bakery window, where Brad was helping Grant pull out the waterlogged flooring. He'd matured a lot over the past few years. He even claimed to be staying in Sunset Cove. She'd been burned too many times to believe him, though.

Avery leaned on the rake and followed Brook's gaze. "They work well together. I'm glad Brad joined Grant Construction. He seems happy to be back." She paused, considering her words. "You both seemed pretty cozy at the shelter. Anything you wanted to tell me?"

Brook snorted, then grunted as she heaved the last large branch to the edge of the sidewalk. The men still needed to move the fallen tree trunk, but at least people could walk past the bakery without tripping on tree branches.

She avoided Avery's question as long as possible, letting the awkward silence stretch between them. Finally, she turned to her friend. "It was nice of him to help clean up the bakery. He seems like a nice guy now. There's nothing going on between us, though."

Avery stared at her friend. "Brad didn't just help you clean up the bakery. He got you out of a flooding town after everyone else was gone. He helped us in the shelter's kitchen." She scooped up a pile of twigs and dropped them into her brother's truck. "Something tells me his helpfulness goes beyond friendship."

"You're overthinking this. We're just friends. Besides, it would be awkward to date your brother now." Not that Brad was unattractive. He'd filled out nicely, working in construction. And he wasn't a terrible kisser. This was just a case of needing to follow her head, not her heart. Her brain was telling her to stay away. There were so many reasons she shouldn't get involved with Brad.

Avery sighed and placed a hand on her non-existent belly.

Brook yanked the rake out of her friend's other hand. "Don't do that. You can't play the wise, pregnant friend already. You're not even showing yet."

She giggled. "Sorry, I can't help it. Here's what I think. I warned Brad to be careful around you. I don't want you to get hurt. But he's changed since moving back. He's calmer. More settled. Maybe you should give him a chance."

The bakery bell ran as Brad stepped outside. "A chance at what?"

Brook shot Avery a dirty look. "It's nothing."

But Avery just smiled sweetly at her brother. "I told Brook to give you a chance. You should go on another date. See if there are any sparks."

Was it Brook's imagination, or did Brad blush? She felt her own face turn red as she thought about the kisses they'd shared during their one and only date. There had been sparks, alright. "We don't need to..." Her voice trailed off. What didn't they need to do? Check for sparks? Get married and live happily ever after? This conversation was taking an awkward turn. She shouldn't need her best friend to find a date for her.

To her surprise, Brad gave her an easy smile. "Avery's right. Let's go out for lunch. No commitments, no pressure."

Brad went inside to help Grant finish the day's work. They needed to remove the drywall and flooring now, before the moisture caused any more mold. Gutting the building shouldn't delay the renovations, as long as they did it now. Brook was grateful to have not one, but two friends she could trust to rebuild her bakery.

As soon as Brad stepped back inside, Brook whirled around to face Avery. "What were you thinking? I'm just friends with your brother. I don't need help finding a new boyfriend."

Avery smiled smugly. "He didn't say no. Besides, I only wanted to be friends with Grant. I'm glad we took the jump into something more. It was scary, but it worked out in the end. I got to marry my best friend."

After everyone left, Brook stood alone in her empty bakery. The building was like a metaphor for her life—gutted, abandoned, and left alone to dry. But unlike her love life, they would rebuild the bakery. Quickly, too, if Grant's intentions said anything.

She looked around the empty shell. From this point forward, she would need Brad. Sure, they'd make all the decisions together. But he would supply the manpower and materials needed to get the job done.

The idea left her feeling vulnerable. She didn't enjoy depending on other people.

Brook rubbed the exhaustion out of her eyes and grabbed her apartment keys. She was lucky to still have a place to stay. They'd stopped the mold from spreading into her apartment. Things could have been a lot worse.

She locked the bakery door and walked up the exterior steps to her home. With each step, she imagined what life would be like if Brad were more than a friend. He hadn't been the best teenage boyfriend, but he seemed different now. Steadier, somehow. Ready to commit to one lucky woman.

If they'd met for the first time this month, she might have snagged him for herself.

Chapter Twenty-Seven

Brad

BRAD SAT AT THE kitchen table, alone. It was too quiet.

Grant had offered his old house until Brad found an apartment. Brad had readily agreed; Avery needed some space with her new family.

He'd spent some time with Grant in this house before the wedding. But without the noise of his sister's family filling the rooms, it seemed empty and lonely.

An incoming text message broke the silence.

> Pastor Rick
>
> Kindness Committee beach cleaning party on Saturday.
>
> RSVP by Friday.
>
> The church will supply lunch and drinks.

Brad looked at the message, surprised. He hadn't realized his number was on the Kindness Committee's phone chain already. Brad still owed Brook a lunch date to catch up—did this count? Hopefully not. He needed a real chance to impress her.

He considered his options, then opened a new text message.

> Brook
>
> Did you hear about the beach clean-up?

> Are you going?

> I'm going. Want a ride to the beach?

> Brook
>
> That's fine. See you Saturday.

Brad turned off his phone and sat back in the kitchen chair. It wasn't a date. It wasn't much of anything. He was just cleaning the beach with her.

Still, spending time with Brook was always a good thing.

The next few days passed quickly. Brad worked with Grant and his crew, repairing the last of the damage in town.

The ocean was a powerful force. They were lucky the storm had spared most of the town, but a few businesses and homes needed major repairs. Brook's bakery had been one of the hardest hit.

He was eager to put Brook's kitchen back together. Brook wouldn't relax until she was busy with customers again. It surprised him to realize how much her happiness mattered to him. Maybe he had grown into a better man.

On Saturday morning, Brad's truck rolled to a stop in front of Seaside Cupcakes. Brook stood on the sidewalk in sturdy jeans and a puffy winter coat. She looks adorable, he thought miserably. He inched further away from friendship and closer to longing every time he saw her.

Brook jumped into the truck, her bright mood like a beam of sunshine compared to his own dark thoughts. "Good morning! It's a great day to clean the beach, don't you think?"

Brad gazed past Brook and out her window. A brilliant sun illuminated the entire town. "It's hard to believe there was so much rain. It's beautiful now." He turned his gaze to Brook. *She could outshine the sun on a summer day*, he thought. His brain felt fuzzy for a moment as warm vanilla drifted toward him. She hadn't baked in days. How did she always smell so wonderful?

She clicked her seatbelt together and turned to grin at him. Her smile dropped a bit when she saw him staring. "Everything okay? Are you ready to go?"

He cleared his throat and nodded, then shifted the truck into drive. "I'm fine. It's been a long time since I've done a beach cleanup, though." They drove to the beach entrance in silence. To Brad's surprise, the parking lot held over twenty vehicles. "It's a good turnout," he said.

Brook smiled and gestured toward Pastor Rick, who was gathering people into groups and giving out instructions. "Even before we formed the Kindness Committee, Sunset Cove was a great place. Neighbors help each other. We want our town to look its best. People always show up for beach cleanings."

Brad climbed out of the truck and rushed over to Brook's door. Before he could help her, she opened her own door and hopped out. She might be short, but she didn't let size stop her from doing anything. Brad had to admit that he liked her attitude.

Still, Brad had hoped for a chance to show off his manners. He chuckled to himself. Brook didn't wait for help if she could do something herself. She was fiercely independent. It was a nice change from the women he'd dated after college. They all expected a man to fix their problems.

Brad grinned and grabbed a roll of trash bags from his truck, then followed Brook toward the crowd.

Pastor Rick was speaking to the group. "If we spread out, we can work faster. No sense having thirty people clean the same space," he explained, motioning to the dozen people who had broken away and headed toward their vehicles. "Brad, I need at least one truck owner in each group. You'll take the far side, past the boardwalk. We'll use your truck to haul trash bags back to the church's dumpsters."

Brad nodded and held up his roll of heavy-duty bags. "I'll go wherever you send me. We're ready to work."

"That's the spirit. You have ten volunteers. Brook, you want to go with Brad?" The pastor paused for a moment as she nodded. "Make that eleven volunteers. Let's meet at the church in two hours for lunch."

Brad felt more cheerful as Brook climbed back into his truck. "Here we go," he said, glad that Brook had joined him. He pointed his truck toward the farthest beach entrance, several blocks away.

This far past the boardwalk, you could drive right onto the sand if you had four-wheel drive. The trick was to keep moving on the softer stretches of sand. He wouldn't take risks today. The storm had caused too much drifting; he didn't want to get stuck. So instead of easing his truck onto the sandy beach, he backed into the entrance and stopped.

Brad's jaw dropped as he climbed out of the truck and gazed at the shoreline. He'd been busy working in town and hadn't checked the beach since the storm. It was a mess. The wind and waves had washed away half of the sand. Debris covered what was left. His heart broke for their beautiful beach.

Brook seemed less upset. She jumped out of the cab and slammed the door, moving straight into no-nonsense mode. She climbed into the truck bed to address their volunteers. "We'll each take one trash bag. Once it's full or too heavy to carry, bring it back to Brad's truck."

She scanned the beach and pointed to volunteers working in the distance. "I can see the next group to our left. The beach ends a quarter-mile to our right. Let's start there and work toward the next group."

Brook jumped down from the truck bed and motioned for Brad to follow her. They marched toward the far side of the public beach and a pile of weather-worn boulders that marked its end.

They worked in silence as they combed the sand, picking up driftwood and garbage. Brad picked up two trash cans that were knocked over. The cans had been empty, their liners and contents dumped and dispersed.

Brook's quick work impressed Brad. She moved rhythmically, picking her way across the sand without breaking stride. She'd done this before. "How often does the town clean the beach?"

"I've helped a few times. There was a bad hurricane our senior year of high school. Avery and I came out with her grandfather to clean up. It was eye-opening. There are millions of pounds of trash in the ocean. If we cleaned up this much, how much is still out there? Anyway, it made an impression on me and showed me how important it is to volunteer."

He nodded, keeping his eyes glued to the sand as he picked up another plastic bottle. Brad remembered that hurricane. He'd started college that year, and had just dated and dumped Brook. He was embarrassed to admit that he'd avoided the town that day.

Instead of helping, he'd hidden in his dorm room to avoid running into Brook.

His gut twisted as he realized how selfish he'd been. He hadn't just let Brook down. He'd also let his grandfather down, and the entire town, just to avoid being uncomfortable.

But if she remembered that part of the story, Brook didn't mention it. She kept her head down and kept working. In fact, her bag was nearly full. Brad's was still half-empty. He pulled himself together and picked up the pace as she continued to talk about past beach cleanings.

"We had a big storm the year the bakery opened, too. No flooding, but we lost a lot of sand from the beach. I helped clean up the driftwood and trash that time, too. I found some pretty sea glass. It's hanging in my bakery." She glanced at him, then averted her eyes as she continued to comb the beach. Her voice hitched as if she might cry. "They were as colorful as a rainbow. I thought it was a good-luck symbol. Rainbows are a sign of God's promise not to flood the world, right? I thought it was a sign that my bakery would be safe."

Brad thought back to the now-gutted bakery, where he'd seen her sea glass hanging near the cash register. She had drilled holes into the glass to make a wind chime of sorts. He imagined them clinking together as customers walked by.

As he tried to think of something comforting to say, Brad glanced down at his feet. Something glittery stuck out of the sand. Brad reached down and pulled out a large piece of blue glass, worn smooth by the waves.

He reached out and touched her arm, then handed her the glass. "How's this for a sign? We're going to rebuild the bakery. I can't guarantee you'll never have another flood, but I can guarantee that I'll get you reopened by spring."

She smiled ruefully and held the glass up to the sunlight. "Isn't sea glass funny? It's just trash beaten up by the ocean. People look for it. They collect it. And it's just pieces of broken bottles. The only difference between trash and sea glass is the smooth edges."

Brook picked up another piece of sharp glass and tucked it inside her trash bag. "That piece didn't have enough time to turn into sea glass, I guess." She paused for a moment, then tied the bag shut. "My bag's full. I'll carry it back and get an empty one. Want to come with me?"

Brad held his own bag out to Brook and shook his head. "Why don't you finish filling my bag? I'll carry this one to the truck. It's got to be heavy."

Brook snorted. "Bags of flour are heavier. I can handle it."

He sighed. Brook still wasn't letting him show off his manners. "I know you can do it yourself, but let me help you."

Brook rolled her eyes, but let Brad swap their bags. "Don't get used to it. I don't accept help from many people."

Brad resisted the urge to roll his own eyes and barked out a laugh as he hefted the heavy bag into his arms. "Noted. I won't offer to help you once we've cleaned everything up. Of course, you can always ask for help. That's a different story." The smile fell from his face as his mood turned more serious. "Call me any time. I'll always be there for you."

She stared at him for a moment with her mouth hanging open, then closed her mouth and twisted her lips in a grin. "This is getting weird. Why don't you take that bag of trash before we declare our undying love?"

Brad forced out a chuckle, then turned his back toward Brook before she could see his pained expressed. What was wrong with him? He knew she was joking. He didn't find it funny, though. If he wasn't careful, he'd fall in love with a woman who prided herself on staying independent—and single.

He carried the trash bag to his truck, noting with surprise that there were several full bags in it already. He'd spent too much time looking at Brook, and not enough time cleaning. That wasn't like him. Brad took pride in being a hard worker and team player.

Brad grabbed two empty trash bags and shook his head in frustration. He thought again about the sea glass he'd found. Did Brook think his sharp edges had softened over the years, or did he need more time to smooth out his edges? He liked to think that he was a different guy now.

As he walked back to Brook, he realized their job was almost done. The twelve of them had quickly cleared the beach, accomplishing what would have taken one person a full day. Within another thirty minutes, his team had finished collecting the trash, tied up their bags, and tossed them into Brad's truck.

Brook jumped into the truck after thanking their volunteers. She turned to face him as they drove toward the church. "Thanks again for picking me up. And thanks for the help. Does this count toward getting to know each other?"

Brad turned to Brook with a thoughtful look. He wasn't letting her get out of their date that easily. "It might. To really get to know each other again, we'll need to visit The Cove."

Brook frowned as she considered the popular outdoor restaurant. "Are they even open? They were so close to the water."

Brad shook his head. "Their kitchen didn't fare better than yours, and the outdoor deck was destroyed. Fortunately, decks are easy enough to replace. Insurance will cover the damage. We'll have them up and running before tourist season. Until then, they'll be using a food truck."

Brook stared out the window as they drove through town. The houses several blocks away from the beach were already looking close to normal. Sand had been swept away and tree limbs removed. The flooding on the roads had receded. A few houses had tarps on their roofs or plywood covering their windows, but most looked like nothing had happened.

The businesses closest to the ocean hadn't been as fortunate.

She turned to Brad with a serious expression. "The Cove's food truck will need our support. Let me know when they open."

He nodded. "It's a date."

She gave him a warning look. "It's not a date."

He grinned and turned his focus back to the road. "Whatever you say, Brook. I'll let you know when they sell milkshakes and burgers again."

Chapter Twenty-Eight

Brook

Brook hummed to herself as she finished cleaning the church's kitchen. She'd take a quick break, then get back to work.

The last few weeks had gone smoothly. Brad and Grant had gutted her bakery, ripping out walls and flooring to prevent any lasting damage. They'd also spent a few days completing their plans for the bakery expansion, taking into account the new lunch menu she hoped to offer.

She was using the church's commercial kitchen until Seaside Cupcakes reopened. She and Avery baked dozens of treats daily, selling them to locals and the occasional tourist who wandered into the church. Brook had hung a sign on the bakery door just two days after they returned to town, directing customers to her temporary kitchen.

They'd had a burst of activity on Valentine's Day weekend, but continued to have a slow and steady customer base. At this rate, the bakery would reopen on solid financial footing. It was more than Brook could have hoped for.

It did her heart good to see the town coming back to life. She had never been more grateful for the residents of Sunset Cove.

She looked up as the door opened and waited for her next customer. Her smile slipped in surprise when she saw Brad stroll toward her, juggling a paper bag and drink carrier. The familiar smell of cheeseburgers drifted into the kitchen.

"Is The Cove open?" she squealed. "You should have told me!"

Brad shrugged and put the bag on the tables Brook set out for her customers. He pulled out four cheeseburgers and popped two chocolate milkshakes out of the drink carrier. "Their new food truck was out today. I wanted to surprise you."

She snatched a milkshake from the table and took a long, satisfying pull. "Oh, I missed these. Were they busy?"

"It was like watching an ice cream truck in August," he joked. "There were twenty people behind me."

"That's fantastic. We've got to support each other."

Brad picked up a burger and bit into it, then wiped his face with a napkin. "I agree, and I knew how much you wanted to support a fellow restaurant owner. That's why I waited in line for you."

The gesture touched Brook. She put down her own burger and walked over to wrap her arms around Brad. "Thank you," she mumbled into his sweatshirt. "This means a lot to me." She clung to him until it felt awkward, but couldn't make herself let go. And his smell... men rarely smelled this good.

She laughed and unwrapped her arms from around his shoulders. "Sorry about that. I really am grateful."

Brad raised his eyebrows. "I'll never turn down a hug from a beautiful woman, especially you."

Happiness, confusion, and a touch of longing swirled through her mind. What was wrong with her? Brook had no right to feel this way about Brad. She picked up her burger again and spoke with her mouth full, covering her mouth in an attempt at manners. "I'm sorry you had to wait in line, but this food is great. Thank you again."

He grinned and finished his own food, crumbling the wrapper and throwing it into the bag. "It's nothing. You wanted something from The Cove, and they were driving by. I'll grab something the next time I see them, too."

She couldn't imagine teenage Brad surprising her with a Cove burger. Generic flowers or candy, maybe. But he'd never stuck around a girl long enough to discover what she liked.

He'd done that now, she realized. He'd listened to her and knew how important she thought it was to support The Cove. This wasn't a date. But it was something. She might even look forward to the lunch date Avery had talked them into.

Brook smiled as she finished her first burger and wiped her mouth. "Can I save the rest for later? I need to get back to work."

"Of course. This way you'll have dinner waiting when you're done."

Brook nodded and gestured for Brad to follow her back into the church's kitchen. She tucked her milkshake and burger into the refrigerator. "Thanks again. I don't get a lot of customers after lunch, but I've got an order to fill today. Someone's picking up three dozen brownies this afternoon. I'm making tomorrow's cupcakes, too."

Brad glanced at the clock, then turned back to Brook. "I've got an hour. Can I help?"

"You were a big help at the shelter, but do you have any baking experience?"

"I helped Avery put cupcake wrappers into the tins," he said, his eyes glimmering with humor.

She threw her head back and laughed. "That's Sophia's job now. Since she's not here, you can help. Go wash your hands."

They worked side by side for the next hour. Once the brownies were in the oven, she switched to cupcakes. As promised, he prepped the tins while she mixed batter and filled each cupcake liner with a piping bag.

Brad stood back to watch her finish the cupcakes and pull the brownies from the oven. They'd worked together before, but he'd always brought his own work to finish while she baked. This felt different. More intimate. With no paperwork in front of him, Brad focused his attention on her instead.

To her surprise, Brad greeted the day's last customers as they wandered into the church. Harry Anderson had been a regular since she'd moved to the church's kitchen. He came at the end of each day, ordering whatever was left over. Brook suspected the man was doing this intentionally, to make sure she didn't waste food or profit.

She smiled as Harry and Brad chatted, knowing that he was about to place his usual request. She pulled the last cupcakes out of the oven and joined them. "What would you like today, Harry? I've got a half-dozen blueberry muffins left, or a dozen chocolate chip cookies."

He appeared to think for a moment, then nodded. "My neighbor's daughter likes blueberry muffins. Give me the half-dozen, and I'll have plenty to share."

She boxed up the muffins and named a price, offering her regular customer a generous discount. Harry handed her a twenty-dollar bill and stuffed his change in the tip jar on the counter.

Brook sighed and shook her head as he walked away. So much for giving him a discount.

Brad watched the transaction with a bemused smile. After Harry left, he turned to Brook. "He's a generous tipper."

"Harry's here every afternoon. He was a regular customer back at the bakery, but he buys my leftover stock now. He's a real sweetheart. It's a nice way to end the day."

Brad looked at the last container of cookies on the counter. "What happens to things that don't sell?"

"Sometimes Pastor Rick takes treats to shut-ins. I've donated trays of cookies to the hospital staff. But I've gotten good at guessing how much I'll sell, especially now. I can't afford to give away a lot of food. Not with the cost of replacing my kitchen and supplies."

He reached into his wallet and pulled out a twenty-dollar bill, then stuffed it into the tip jar next to Harry's change. "I'm taking the cookies. They look delicious, and Harry's got the right idea. I'm sure Avery and Sophia will share them with me."

Brook laughed as she wrapped up the cookies. "Avery baked them this morning, but I'm sure you'll make Sophia happy. Grant likes the chocolate chip cookies, too." She turned to face Brad. He was staring at the floor with his hands in his pockets. "What's wrong?"

"I'm glad you've got people like Harry to support you. I should have been inside your bakery on the first day it opened. We were friends, and maybe something more. I should have stayed around and showed that I cared about your business. That I cared about you."

Brook sucked in a deep breath and rocked back on her heels. This conversation had taken a deeper turn than she'd expected. "If you were living here, I'm sure you would have visited the bakery. You were busy with life. I can understand that."

"You're too nice. I deserve to be kicked out of town for the way I treated you." Brad cleared his throat. "I'm still hoping to make it up to you. At least the town took care of you, even when I didn't."

Brook hesitated, trying to sort out the jumble of emotions in her head. He'd all but abandoned her after their first date, leaving her alone and confused. In hindsight, she knew Brad had been equally scared. He'd had a tough childhood. Losing his parents, moving to a new town to live with his grandfather. She could understand why commitment was hard for him.

She reached out and squeezed his hand. "Sunset Cove takes care of its own. If you'd stayed, they'd have taken care of you, too."

Brad sighed and lifted his head, looking Brook in the eyes. "I have a lot of regrets, and leaving is my biggest one. I wish I'd stayed. Build a life here. But I can't change the past."

"No, you can't. But you can change your future," Brook said brightly, trying to shift the mood. "You're staying in Sunset Cove. You're helping us rebuild. And I can see cookie dough ending up in your fridge soon. If you're willing to help, of course. Cookie dough solves many problems."

Brad's sad eyes brightened at the mention of his favorite treat. He allowed her to change the subject back to baking, leaving their serious conversation behind. Brook knew they'd need to finish that talk later. This afternoon, though, it was time to finish their work and have some fun.

"Grab the heat-treated flour from the pantry," she ordered. "We'll need it if I want to save some raw dough. I've got pasteurized eggs, too." Today called for comfort food. Brook measured each of the ingredients out and mixed them together, swatting away Brad's hand when he tried to sneak a taste.

Once she divided the dough between the refrigerator and a small bowl next to Brad's coat, he helped clean the kitchen. Brook gave a sigh of relief when the last bowl was washed. She slumped onto a folding chair. "What a day. Time to get off my feet."

Brad dragged a box from the recycling pile over to her chair. "Prop your feet up. You deserve a break."

She put up her feet, then leaned back in the chair and yawned. "Thanks for coming in today. It's lonely here sometimes, especially after Avery leaves."

"Glad to help." He smiled, then glanced down at his phone. "I need to grab some things from Pastor Rick's office. We're filling Easter eggs today. Can you believe we're still having the egg hunt?"

Nothing could keep the residents of Sunset Cove down for long—not even a flood. "Why didn't you say something? My last customer should be here soon, but I can fill eggs while I'm waiting."

She had barely gotten the words out when the church door opened. Avery, Grant, and Rachel spilled into the hallway.

Guilt colored Brad's face. "We're working in the hall. I hope that's okay. We needed room to spread out, and the candy was already here. But you've had a long day. I don't expect you to help."

Brook held back a sigh. What was a few more hours of work? Besides, she wasn't ready to say goodbye to Brad. She was surprised to realize how much she enjoyed his company. "I can put my feet up while I fill eggs. I can't leave until my brownie pickup comes, anyway."

By this time, their friends had entered the kitchen. Rachel wrapped her friend in a hug. "It's so good to see you. I'm sorry I haven't stopped by."

Brook gave her friend a hug back. "You've been busy. I'm sure the kids are happy to be back at school."

Rachel snorted. "Most wouldn't mind if we stayed closed. We've got so much fun planned for spring, though." After reviewing their options, the Kindness Committee would hold the egg hunt at the school. There would be plenty of room for everyone.

Brook's eyes widened as Brad and Grant walked down the hallway with two large totes, each topped with bags of candy. "How many eggs are you filling today?"

Brad slid a tote onto the closest table and began unloading candy. "As many as we can. Easter is a few weeks away, but we've got a lot of work to do."

Avery nodded her head, looking concerned. "We'll need all the time we can get. That's not five thousand eggs, though. Wasn't that how many Pastor Rick wanted us to fill?"

"He's got eight more totes of empty eggs," Brad said, shifting his feet and avoiding his sister's eyes. "Plenty for every kid. You were right. This is a huge project."

Brook groaned and pulled out a chair in front of the empty eggs. She'd told Brad it was a mistake to volunteer for the egg hunt committee. Still, she wouldn't make her friends work alone. The five friends chatted as they split open plastic eggs and slid candy inside each one, dropping the filled eggs back into a tote.

Brook was opening the last bag of candy when her customer arrived. He paid for his brownies and thanked her for making them on such short notice. It was his son's fifth birthday, he explained. Their home had flooded, and there wasn't time to plan a party. At least his son could have his favorite treat.

Her heart felt heavy as she walked back to her friends. People were still piecing their lives together in Sunset Cove.

In the time it took her to sell the brownies, her friends finished filling the eggs. Brook slumped into her chair and pasted a tired smile on her face. "You all did an amazing job."

Rachel eyed her friend with concern. "You helped too, but are you okay? You don't look so great."

Brook rubbed her eyes and tried to keep the exhaustion out of her voice. "It's been a long week. I never realized how convenient it was to live above my business. I'm still close enough to walk home, but it's hard." Even as she spoke, she knew that moving the bakery was only part of her problem. Watching the town struggle, her mixed-up feelings for Brad—her brain felt like it was about to short-circuit and shut down.

Brad squeezed her shoulder as he walked by, then picked up the totes filled with eggs. "I'm taking these to the office, then driving you home. No walking tonight. Grant, can you help?"

She watched him leave and held back a sigh. Brad really was a nice guy. Why were things so confusing? She wished, just once, that she could meet a guy with no past, no reason to hesitate. She was tired of being lonely.

Rachel watched her gaze with a barely-concealed grin. "So... how's it going with Brad? I heard you're going out for lunch soon."

Brook dropped her head to the table. The last thing she needed was her friends' scrutiny. "Does everyone know about that?" she mumbled.

Avery shrugged and offered a sheepish smile. "Not everyone. Just a few friends. Rachel knows, plus Kerry and Emma. Oh, and Grant. He might have told Nick. That should be it."

Brook giggled. What a ridiculous situation. There was no privacy in a small town.

The giggle turned into a snort, and by the time Brad and Grant had returned, the women were laughing until tears ran down their cheeks.

The men glanced at each other. Grant shrugged. "I love them all, but our women are a little strange."

Brook just managed to hear his comment over the laughter. She'd never liked when a man claimed her as "his woman," but still felt a stab of loneliness. She wanted to belong with someone. To find a partner in life, as Avery had worded it.

If she found a man to spend her life with, wouldn't it be nice to be friends with him first?

It was a shame things were so complicated with Brad.

Chapter Twenty-Nine

Brad

Brad put down the hammer and stood back to admire his work.

He'd worked in construction for ten years, but this was his first time leading a project from start to finish. He was proud of himself.

The storm had stretched their crew thin. It had challenged Brook, too. She couldn't work in her kitchen yet, but she'd started selling food from the front of her shop again. At least the customers' area was finished and inspected.

With the front of the bakery finished, Avery came in each day to sell food made at the church. Brook baked across town until Avery's shift ended. It was an awkward arrangement, one that required the women to drive across town multiple times each day. Still, he knew Brook was pleased with his work. He lived for those moments when she walked through the kitchen door, beaming at his progress. He enjoyed making her feel happy.

But when the kitchen door flew open this morning, it wasn't Brook's smiling face that greeted him. Instead, Avery marched into the kitchen and squared herself in front of her brother, her arms folded. "How much longer will this take?" she demanded. "I can't stand one more drive to the church. Honestly, the smell of cupcakes in my car is making me…" Her face turned a delicate shade of green. "Be right back."

He watched with concern as Avery rushed out the door and into the customers' bathroom. The sound of retching filled the bakery. Brad shook his head. He didn't know how much longer his sister and Brook could keep this up. They were both wearing themselves thin, and Avery's pregnancy hormones didn't help.

Brad unbuckled his tool belt and went to the finished side of the bakery to check on Avery. He knocked on the door. "Are you okay? Can I get you anything?"

"Give me a minute. Find me a bottle of water, please."

Brad dashed to the kitchen toward Brook's new, larger refrigerator. They couldn't store food for sale in it yet, not until the kitchen was inspected. At least they could keep water cold. He grabbed a bottle for Avery and rushed back to the bathroom.

She stood outside the bathroom, leaning her head against the closed door. "Thanks," she said, reaching for the bottle of water. She took a few pulls, then gave her brother a weak smile.

"Sorry I'm so grumpy. I know you're working as fast as you can."

Brad nodded. "I was waiting for Brook to update both of you. We'll hook up the appliances this week. I've called the gas guy and scheduled time with our electrician. We're on the last stretch."

Relief filled Avery's face as she walked over to the new dining booths they'd just installed. She eased into a seat, taking care to protect her barely-visible bump. "That's great news. Brook works too hard, trying to be in two places at once. She's grateful for you, though. She's just afraid to say it. I think she's afraid you'll take it the wrong way."

"Afraid I'll take what the wrong way?" Brook asked, pushing open the door between the kitchen and the dining area. "Brad, the kitchen looks great. Are the appliances ready yet?" She rubbed her hands together, her eyes gleaming with excitement. "I can't wait to bake in the oven we picked out."

Avery cleared her throat. "Brad will get the appliances and gas hooked up this week. That means you'll have time to go on that lunch date."

Brook blinked. "That came out of nowhere."

"It's the pregnancy hormones," Brad explained. "She's been blurting things out all week. Thanks, Avery, but we don't need your help."

Avery crossed her arms and narrowed her eyes. "You agreed to a date. You've been flirting and smiling at each other for weeks. I've seen the way you look at her when she's not watching. And Brook, tell me you're not admiring him when he works in your kitchen."

Brook's face flushed. "What are you talking about?"

Avery took off her apron and flung it on the table. "I'm going home. Sophia will be home soon, and I've got to get supper started. Brook, do you need anything else from me?"

Brook looked at her best friend, confusion filling her face. "I'm finished baking for the day. Brad can help with the boxes in my car. We're fine until tomorrow morning."

Avery nodded. "I'll see you tomorrow at the church. You need some time alone."

Brad stared at his sister as she walked out the door and began the short walk home. He had planned to ask Brook out on a date soon. They'd just been so busy with the renovations.

He'd listened to Nick's advice and worked on being a reliable friend. Brad made a point of touching base with her at the end of each day. He enjoyed spending a few quiet minutes together, talking about the bakery's progress and asking about her day.

It wouldn't take a big push to fall in love with Brook. He'd been halfway there as a teen, and she'd grown into an amazing woman. Brad hoped she could see how much he'd matured, too.

He said nothing as they stood there alone. Instead, he searched Brook's eyes, wondering what she'd thought about Avery's little speech. He hoped the reminder about their date hadn't made Brook uncomfortable. Brad had a few surprises lined up for today, and he didn't want his sister's comments to derail them.

"Why don't I show you today's progress?" he asked, holding out his hand. He wrapped his hand around hers as he tugged her toward the kitchen, enjoying her small hand in his more than he cared to admit. "I've got the foundation built for your countertops. There's extra space, since I know you want to prep lunches. There's room to make sandwiches or sides while someone else bakes."

He stopped at a gap in the woodwork. "Here's the space for your oven. We'll get everything hooked up and installed this week. Then we can slide the counters into place and get you open for business."

Brook's eyes teared up as she looked around the kitchen. "It's coming together. Thank you. It couldn't have been easy getting this done so quickly."

"It was important to me. You're important to me, too." He glanced down at their hands, which were still linked, then tugged her across the kitchen. "Your commercial fridge came last week. Have you used it yet?"

"We can't store food for sale until the health department inspects the kitchen."

He tugged her closer and nodded toward the door handle. "Open the doors. Check it out."

She laughed and shook her head, pulling her hand out of his grasp. "I've seen the inside. It's perfect. It's bigger than the old one, with more shelving."

Brad huffed out a breath and ran his hand through his hair. "Just open the door, Brook."

She tilted her head and stared at him for a moment, then reached for the handle and opened the refrigerator. Brook frowned as she pulled out a bouquet of roses. "What are these for?"

He spun Brook toward him so they were face-to-face. "You've been working so hard, and I thought you'd like flowers in your apartment. They always made you happy." He paused and considered the best path forward. He'd gotten the flowers to cheer her up, but there was no sense holding back. "I still owe you a date. I'm sorry that I hurt you when we were kids, but will you give me a second chance?

Brad held his breath as she stared at the flowers warily. Had he pushed too hard?

"A second chance at what?"

Brad's lips mashed together. He hadn't expected this to be so awkward. Of course, Brook had every right to be cautious. Brad needed to make his intentions clear. "A second chance at dating. A chance for us to see… If I hadn't been an idiot, maybe we would've worked out. I'd like to try."

She looked down at the flowers hanging limply in her hands. "Oh," she whispered.

His stomach clenched as he watched a range of emotions wash over Brook's face. Surprise, sadness, and the hint of a smile. He held on to that smile and fought down a sense of panic. As much as he wanted to date Brook, he didn't want to hurt their friendship, either. If trying to date her meant he could lose her completely, he'd take it all back. "We don't have to do this. I've changed, though. We both have. We might be good together now, but it's okay if you don't want to find out."

Brook brought the flowers to her nose and inhaled deeply. She nodded. "I should have called or texted when you left. I shouldn't have let you walk away without asking 'why.' So let's do it. One date. But most of my dates end in disaster. If that happens to us, we won't let it destroy our friendship. Agreed?"

"My dates don't end in disaster," Brad reassured her. "You're right, though. No matter what happens, no one walks away. We stay friends."

He took an instinctive step forward, drawn toward Brook and the delicate smell of her perfume. She still smelled like vanilla, but now she smelled like her bakery again—vanilla with a hint of cocoa powder and the sweet treats she loved so much. The smell went straight to his head.

He wanted to kiss her so badly, but stopped himself. Now wasn't the time. If he tried anything now, he might scare her away.

Brad would save his best moves for their first date.

Chapter Thirty

Brook

Brook grinned as she walked into the conference room at Grace Lutheran Church. It had been an uneventful day, but she had big plans tonight. First there was a Kindness Committee meeting. Then she'd finish the night with Brad, going straight from the meeting to their date.

Nearly twenty people sat around the table with bags of candy in front of them. Easter was just two weeks away, and the big egg hunt was next Saturday.

As she settled into the seat next to Avery, Pastor Rick walked into the room with Grant and Brad. They each had a tote that rattled with empty plastic eggs.

The pastor slid his tote in front of Harry and another elderly man. "Here you go, men. This one's for the three of us."

Harry scooped out a handful of eggs and started working. "Let's see how quickly we can fill these eggs. I hear Brad's got somewhere important to be tonight. The faster we finish up, the faster he can leave." He turned to wink at Brad.

Brook held back a grown. Did the whole town know about their date?

Of course, having a town filled with people who cared wasn't horrible. She wouldn't have survived the storm if the town hadn't supported her business. She heard The Cove's food truck had been busy, too. The town had taken care of its people.

Harry looked over at Avery and Brook with a cheeky grin. "The race is on, ladies. I hear Brook's got plans, too. You better fill those eggs fast."

Brook laughed and reached inside the tote Brad had placed in front of her.

He put a hand on her shoulder. "Don't worry, I've got lots of experience filling eggs. We'll get this done in time. I've got a surprise for tonight."

Brad wasn't joking about the experience. She sat down with him every night this week after he finished working at the bakery. They talked a bit as they worked on the eggs, filling in the gaps of their past. So much had happened in the decade they'd been apart. It had been nice to catch up.

Brook could see how badly his sister's first marriage had messed with him. He'd watched her suffer through a toxic relationship, and Avery's ex-husband had cut Brad off from his family. Now that she was divorced, Brad could finally claim his status as uncle. He might stick around this time. Maybe not for her, but definitely for his sister and Sophia.

The committee chatted as they worked through the last of the eggs. With so many people working together, they finished quickly. Pastor Rick carried the last tote to his office, the filled eggs clacking together. When he returned, he smiled at the group. "Many hands make light work! Now, let's discuss the egg hunt and your assigned stations."

He walked to the whiteboard and split the committee members into groups. "Brook and Brad, you're in charge of the playground. You'll hide eggs for the older kids and supervise them. You'll have Harry to help you."

The pastor assigned Avery and Grant to the Clint Brown Kindness Fund table. Any donations collected at the egg hunt would buy school supplies for next year.

Pastor Rick would supervise the church youth group and the remaining volunteers at the football field.

Brook raised her hand as the pastor wrapped things up. "Rachel doesn't come to meetings, but she's willing to help. She's a teacher and can get inside the building if we need anything."

Pastor Rick nodded. "That's a great idea. Let's put her at the playground. Does anyone else have questions? We won't meet again until after the egg hunt."

When no one spoke, he led them through a brief prayer to end the meeting. As they all unfolded their hands and raised their heads, he smiled directly at Brad and Brook. "Have fun with your surprise, Brook."

Brook laughed as they stepped out into the brisk spring air. "Am I the only person who doesn't know where we're going?"

"I didn't tell Harry," Brad said, winking at Brook. "Not everyone knew, but I had to call in some favors. Besides, the pastor says he knows everything that happens in this town. Trust me, you'll like this surprise."

Because they'd each driven to the meeting, Brook needed to take her car home. Brad followed. He was waiting outside his truck, holding the door open for her as she approached him.

She raised her eyebrows. "You're holding doors open now."

"I've been trying to show off my manners since I came back, but you're always too fast for me. Tonight, I open the doors. I know you've had a lot of bad dates. Let's make this a good one."

Brook bit her lip, unsure whether this date was a good idea. She knew Brad was a nice guy. She cared about him. What if they messed everything up? She'd be heartbroken if things went so badly that they couldn't be friends anymore. "No matter what happens, we won't end the night hating each other. Right?"

He leaned in and gave her a gentle kiss on the forehead. "I never hated you, Brook. I was afraid to admit that I cared about you. Because I'm a fool, I ran away. But I could never hate you."

She blushed, then took his hand and let him help her into the truck. Once they were on the road, she cleared her throat. "I didn't hate you, either. We shouldn't have avoided each other for so many years. I let my pride, and my busy life, get in the way of our friendship."

Brad nodded. "Tonight's a night for second chances. We both have regrets. Let's forget everything that's happened in the past. Today's a new day."

To her surprise, Brad was already pulling the truck to the side of the road. They hadn't gone far, just a few blocks. He pulled the truck into park and held out his hand. "Wait one minute. I'm opening your door tonight, remember?"

He walked around and opened her door.

"We're at the end of the boardwalk," she said slowly. "There's nothing out here, except..." Brook was interrupted by the lights of The Cove restaurant as they flickered on, filling the sidewalk with a soft glow. She gasped. "They're not open yet. They can't be."

Brad grinned and stuck his hands in his coat pockets, looking sheepish. "We finished their kitchen two days ago, and they wanted to open for the two of us. The owner was excited to make this surprise happen. I thought you'd like this more than a restaurant out of town."

His thoughtfulness touched Brook. She leaned toward him, wrapping her arms around his waist. "There aren't a lot of restaurant owners in Sunset Cove, so we stick together. Thanks for remembering."

Some of her excitement faded as she looked out toward the sand. The small kitchen stood proud and ready, with a fresh coat of paint. But beyond that, there was nothing.

Gone were the bustling crowds, their favorite table where they'd gathered after class in high school. Gone were the wind-smoothed planks of wood. Sand dunes and grasses were all that remained. They'd done their job of protecting the shore, but they'd failed to keep the restaurant and deck safe.

If Brad sensed her emotions, he didn't respond. He reached for her hand and led her across the sand. Someone, probably from Grant Construction, had cleaned up the mess. A solitary picnic table was set up on the sand. A small space heater and lamp stood beside it, offering warmth and light to anyone who sat at the table.

"We'll rebuild the deck next week," he assured her. "For now, you get the table with the best view."

The two of them sat together on the same bench, facing the sunset. A waiter came out moments later with all of their favorite foods from The Cove, including two burgers and chocolate milkshakes. "I hope you don't mind," Brad said. "I ordered our usual. This way we can eat while we watch the show."

It was a good plan, she realized. They enjoyed their food and chatted while the sun gave a spectacular performance. It sank lower in the sky until it seemed to disappear into the waves with a burst of color. Brook sighed and turned toward Brad as the last of the sun's rays faded into darkness. "That was beautiful. Thank you."

Too soon, the waiter came out to clear their table. He brought out cups of coffee and urged them to stay as long as they wanted.

Brad and Brook kept talking, first about The Cove's renovations and then about the bakery's plans. He shared Grant's plans to restore an older Victorian home over the summer and Sophia's excitement about becoming a big sister. When they ran out of words, she leaned into him and enjoyed the sound of the waves.

The moon was glowing when she realized how late it must be. Brook reluctantly sat up and reached for her purse. "We should go. The kitchen staff will want to get home."

Brad smiled and held up a key ring. "They're already home. We've got contractor privileges right now. The owner said to stay as long as we wanted. We just need to lock up."

Once again, Brook was touched by his thoughtfulness. She knew what it was like to stay past closing time for a customer. It was nice of him to arrange for the kitchen staff to go home. She didn't argue when Brad put his arm around her and pulled her back toward him. They sat nestled together, watching the dark waves lap against the shore.

It felt like hours before Brad gave her a squeeze and stood up. "I've got to get up early tomorrow, and you do, too." He walked toward the heater and lamp, turning them both off so that they stood in darkness.

The intimacy of the scene struck Brook. No one would interrupt them out there. Still, Brad was a perfect gentleman. He gave her another kiss on the forehead, then led her back to the truck. Once she was inside the cab, he turned off the kitchen lights and locked up.

They drove the short distance to her house in silence. He hopped out of the truck one last time and opened the door for her, helping her onto the sidewalk in front of the bakery. "I had a nice time," he said.

"Me too. I'm glad we finally went on a date."

After one last kiss, Brook all but floated up the stairs to her apartment. It was the nicest date she'd had in years. With Brad, of all people! If she let herself fall in love, it wouldn't be a far fall. She was nearly there already.

Brook hummed to herself as she changed into sweatpants and settled in for the night. Brad was right—she'd have another early morning tomorrow. She thought back to their evening and smiled. She might be tired tomorrow, but it had been a great day.

But as she went through her routine, the charm of the night started to wear off. She watched the smile on her face melt away as she brushed her teeth. In the mirror, she saw the stern brow she'd inherited from her father. Long, dark hair that matched her mother's. Tears threatened as she thought back to the nights she'd heard her parents argue before their divorce. Every awful date she'd had in high school and beyond flashed before her eyes—including the date where Brad had left town afterward, and never returned.

What had she been thinking? Any relationship with her couldn't end well. It was in her blood. She needed to stop things with Brad before anything bad happened.

The thought made her heart feel like it was breaking in two. A small voice in her head whispered that it was okay to be scared, but it was also okay to love someone like Brad. He'd changed, and he was a better man.

That voice couldn't talk over the fear in her heart.

Chapter Thirty-One

Brad

BRAD GRUNTED AS HE hefted the last piece of granite countertop into place. He nodded at Grant, who had come to help finish the bakery. "Thanks again. That was a two-man job."

Grant nodded and smoothed his hand over the countertop. "Even if you're leading projects, you don't always have to work alone."

It had been weeks since Brad had worked with the rest of the crew. "How's everyone doing? Besides The Cove's deck, this should be the last flood repair on your list."

"Things are slowing down. Nick's done with the smaller projects. We've got two roof repairs to wrap up, but we'll turn our attention to the hospital expansion soon. We'll start once they've framed the new wing."

Brad was looking forward to working on the hospital. It had been a while since he'd worked as part of a big crew. Grant's team was smaller than he was used to, but they'd be pairing up with several construction companies to get the hospital done on deadline.

It was exciting to see his town grow—and even more exciting to have a hand in its growth. Brad hadn't felt nearly as proud of his work out in Pittsburgh. The buildings he'd worked on had been buildings, and nothing more. They weren't the homes and businesses of people he cared about.

The new hospital expansion would include a pediatric wing, which meant better care for the children in Sunset Cove. Better care for Sophia and his new niece or nephew. He was excited to play a role in bringing something so important to his town. More than ever, he knew he'd committed to Sunset Cove for life. His family and job were here. Brook was here, too.

While he was glad Brook's bakery was almost finished, he'd miss working here. Brad had spent a lot of hours in this kitchen, helping Brook's dreams come true. They'd spent time in the dining area too, filling Easter eggs and unwinding after a long day.

Would he have the chance to do that once the bakery was open? Stop by after work, slide into a bench, and catch up with Brook?

Not that he'd seen much of Brook this week. It was strange. They'd had a great date, and she'd disappeared. He'd texted her once, not wanting to seem pushy or like he was ignoring her. All he'd gotten back was a brief reply: Yes, she'd had fun. Yes, she'd be at the egg hunt.

Avery hadn't mentioned Brook to him, other than noting that she'd gotten to work late after their date. It seemed like Brook was knee deep in dough right now, but surely she could text him.

Look at me, becoming the paranoid one, he thought. *She's not ghosting me. She's busy.* He couldn't shake off the feeling that something was wrong, though.

He watched as Grant scrolled through his phone, checking messages and replying to texts. It was the perfect time to pick Grant's brain. "Has Avery said anything about Brook?"

"No, she hasn't. Why?"

"I haven't seen her since our date. I thought it went well, but maybe she didn't enjoy it as much as I thought."

Grant turned off his phone, tucked it in a pocket, and turned his attention to his friend. "It's okay to give women some space. Avery needed space, too. She got scared, especially after I said that I loved her. Make sure Brook knows you're still here, waiting for her to take the next step."

Brad nodded. "I'm trying to be patient. And like I told Brook, I'm not going anywhere. I found a house that's going up for sale. It's too big for one person, but I don't plan to live alone forever."

Grant slapped him on the back and grinned. "Good for you. Let me know if you need help with the home inspection." He picked up his clipboard and headed toward the front door of the bakery. "I'll talk to you soon. I've got a hospital blueprint to approve."

Brad watched his friend and boss leave, then pulled out his own phone.

> Let's do lunch after the egg hunt.

Brook

> We'll be tired after herding all those kids.

> I'm up for coffee.

Brad waited for a minute, staring at the phone while he urged her to reply. When no new messages came, he turned off the screen and shoved the phone in his pocket. This was karma coming back to haunt him. He'd walked out on Brook all those years ago. Now she was the one backing away.

It hurt to be left behind.

Chapter Thirty-Two

Brook

Brook glanced at the clock in her apartment. She grabbed a sweater, threw it on, and rushed out the door.

She was running late. Brook Reed was never late. She was the epitome of responsibility and punctuality. Except for this week. This week, she'd been a sobbing mess.

Brook hadn't seen Brad since their date. She'd see him today at the egg hunt, and she was dreading it. Part of her wanted to run into his arms and wrap him in a hug, give him a big kiss, and apologize for avoiding him all week. They'd work it out, make up, and life would be peachy.

But life didn't work that way. People got hurt. She needed to tell Brad that she was putting their friendship clause into effect. No more dating. Just friendship. She couldn't risk anything more.

She didn't know how to look him in the eyes and claim she wasn't in love, but she had to. It was for his own good. She'd lie about loving him before they both got hurt again.

Her heart sank as she parked next to the school and saw Brad, Harry and Rachel joking together while they hid eggs. They made a good team. Harry pushed around a cart filled with hundreds of eggs, and Brad and Rachel funneled the eggs to their hiding places. The kids would have a blast when they got here. Brook couldn't say the same about herself.

She swallowed the lump in her throat and rushed over to greet them. "Sorry I'm late. What can I do?"

"You look pretty today, Ms. Brook," Harry said as he turned to wink at Brad. "You're a lucky man."

Brad cleared his throat and frowned. "We're almost done hiding the eggs. I thought we could do a scramble for the big kids, too. Dump the rest of the eggs onto the field next to the playground."

Brook looked at the field, where a few patches of mud dotted the lawn. She shook her head. "You'll have kids running around in the mud and falling. Let's keep them on the mulch. The younger kids are running around on artificial turf. We shouldn't have the older ones in the mud, either."

"Good call. Okay, Harry. Where are we hiding the rest of these eggs?"

The older man pointed to a row of hedges next to the sidewalk. "We haven't put them in the hedges yet. I loved finding eggs there as a youngster." The four of them walked over to the hedges and dispersed the rest of the eggs into, on top of, and under the hedges.

They finished a few minutes before the kids would arrive. Brook turned to Brad. "Can we talk? In private?"

Brad shoved his hands into his pockets. "I know what you'll say. Let's wait until after the egg hunt."

She took a deep breath and shook her head. "It can't wait. I just wanted to say that I care about you, but I don't know if I can be with you. We can't do this." Her lip trembled as the words rushed out of her mouth.

Brad slumped over in defeat, then put his hand up. "Let's pause this conversation. I won't pressure you either way, but we shouldn't decide right now. Let's go for coffee. Somewhere quiet, where we can talk."

He stopped talking when Avery tapped him on the shoulder. "I'm sorry. Am I interrupting something?" she asked.

"We were making plans for after the egg hunt," Brad said. "What do you need?"

"Pastor Rick needs someone to run to the bank. We need change for the raffle. Grant won't let me go, and he won't leave me behind." She shook her head. "He's grown very protective of the baby."

Brook watched as he walked away with his sister. Back at the kindness table, Grant pulled out a chair for Avery and handed her a bottle of water. The simple gesture ripped yet another fracture through her already-broken heart. What was it like to care so much about someone that you couldn't leave their side?

She took a tentative step toward Brad's truck. Maybe she could ask if he wanted company at the bank. Then she stopped.

It would already hurt too much when she walked away. Best to ease out of this relationship now, before they got in too deep.

Brook knew she was being silly. It was too late to protect her heart.

She felt better as the egg hunt got underway. It was tough to be sad while dozens of children raced around the playground, cheering as they found each egg. Rachel and Brad joined her at the edge of the grass to watch.

"Is this what recess looks like?" Brook joked. "This is a little crazy. Fun, but crazy."

Rachel laughed. "During the school day, they take turns at recess. They aren't all outside at once."

Brook chuckled as she watched one of the oldest boys help a younger sibling. The size difference between the kids amazed her. Some were nearly as tall as her, while others looked as young as Sophia. She knew Sophia and the youngest kids were at the football field. Still, it cheered her up to watch the kids help each other. Brook had been an only child. If she was ever blessed with children, she hoped they would be as kind as these two boys.

Not that children are likely to happen, she thought. *I need a husband before I can have children, and it's not looking good.*

Brad might be willing, a tiny voice whispered in her head. Brook ignored the idea, but it wasn't easy to push aside thoughts about Brad while he was standing next to her.

Brad elbowed Brook to get her attention. He grinned and pointed out the younger kids in the far-off football field. They walked through the muddy grass together to get a better view. She could see the tiny children running, shrieking, scrambling as they rushed to pick eggs off the ground, while Grant and Avery stood cheering them on. "Sophia's having fun. Aren't you glad we got involved?" he asked.

Brook had to agree. She gave him an awkward smile. "Okay, you were right. I'm sorry I doubted you. I'm glad we filled five thousand eggs, even if it took an entire month."

Brad chuckled. "It was worth it. I'm going to help the kids make sure they didn't miss any eggs. But we're going to talk afterward. It'll be okay."

He gave her a quick kiss on the forehead and jogged back to the playground. Brook had just opened her mouth to remind him about the mud when she saw him slip.

Her heart jumped into her throat. Time seemed to stand still as he flew through the air. A loud CRACK echoed across the field as he landed hard on his left side.

Brook gasped and rushed over to Brad. A thin sheen of sweat covered his face. "Are you okay?"

He tried to sit up and stopped, gasping as he put pressure on his left leg. "I'm not sure. It hurts. My ankle."

"I need help!" Brook yelled, drawing the attention of every child and adult nearby.

Rachel took one look at Brad and dashed toward the parking lot. She returned less than a minute later, driving her SUV through the grass. Kids and parents stopped to stare as she pulled up to Brad. She helped Brook prop him up between them and get him into the vehicle. Once Brook had strapped him in, they rushed toward the hospital.

Four hours later, the three friends were ready to leave the emergency room. Brad had a black cast and a shiny new set of crutches.

Guilt overwhelmed Brook as she looked at Brad. He was one of the kindest, most generous souls she'd ever met. Sure, he'd hurt her once, a long time ago. But he'd been working hard the past few months to prove that he'd changed.

Seeing him in that hospital bed made her realize how foolish her concerns had been. It was too late to protect her heart. She was already in love with Brad. They'd figure out how to keep each other safe. Together.

She brushed the hair off his face and forced a smile. "I'm so sorry this happened. We'll get you back on your feet. You helped me. Now I'll help you."

He looked at her with dazed eyes. The pain medication had gone straight to his head. "I thought you were breaking up with me."

Brook shook her head. "Don't worry about that. We'll get through this."

The emergency room nurse soon came in with discharge paperwork. But they wouldn't leave that easily. As the three of them hobbled toward the exit, a doctor came rushing toward them.

"Doctor Scott Hart," he said, reaching out to shake Brook's and Rachel's hands. He nodded at Brad, then turned his attention to Rachel. "I hope you won't mind the intrusion. I heard you work at the school?"

Rachel nodded, her eyes wide as he gave her a handsome smile.

"I'm in charge of the hospital expansion, and I'd like to partner with the school to raise money. Can I give you my number?" He gestured toward her phone.

Rachel silently handed him the phone and watched as the doctor texted himself.

"There! Now we both have each other's information. I'll be in touch soon." He nodded, gave her another smile, and walked away.

Brook smirked at her friend's expression. Laughing didn't seem like an appropriate response, given everything that had happened today, but she couldn't help herself. Rachel looked dumbfounded. "That doctor didn't want help with the fundraiser. He wanted your number."

"You think so?"

"Trust me, he didn't chase you down the hall because you were a teacher. All he had to do was call the school if he needed help."

Rachel put her hands on her hips and attempted to look stern, but no amount of "teacher authority" could hide her blush. "He did not want my phone number."

"We'll see," Brook sang. "He was handsome, though. What do you say, Brad?"

Brad shook his head, still looking dazed from the pain medication. "You're much prettier than the doctors."

Chapter Thirty-Three

Brook

Brook sat on the couch in Brad's house. Brad was fast asleep, his head resting in her lap. She stroked his hair and wondered how she'd fallen in love with him.

Maybe it was all the takeout from The Cove food truck, or their romantic dinner on the beach.

Maybe it was his dedication to the town. He'd spent countless hours helping Sunset Cove recover from the storm, and still found time to fill thousands of eggs for the local egg hunt.

It might be from realizing how much he'd changed, from a rebellious teen to a caring, considerate man. Or maybe it was the incredible fear she'd felt at the school playground. She'd watched him fall, and her only instinct was to help him. Keep him safe. She'd rushed toward him, all thoughts of her own safety and fear of slipping gone.

Maybe that's what love meant—putting someone else first, and caring for them as much as you cared about yourself.

Brad stirred under her hands. His eyes slowly blinked open. When he saw Brook was still there, his face bloomed with a smile. "You stayed."

"I stayed."

Epilogue

Brook flipped the sign on her bakery door from "closed" to "open." Her heart gave a little thrill. After weeks of hard work, and lots of support from the community, Seaside Cupcakes was open for business.

She walked over to the booth where Brad rested his broken ankle. She leaned in and gave him a soft kiss on the lips. Then she squealed a little sound of joy. "We're finally open! And it's all thanks to you. I'm so glad you came back into our lives. Not because you fixed my bakery," she amended, turning serious. "I love you."

Brad pulled her in for a second kiss. "I love you, too. I'm glad I could help. And I'm so proud of you."

She bounced happily in her seat, taking care not to bump into his cast. "The bakery's done. You're taking some time off until your ankle heals. What's our next adventure?"

"That's your call. Are we taking this slow, or do you want me to move like Grant?"

She laughed and cocked her head. "What are you talking about?"

"If I move as fast as Grant, you could have an engagement ring on your finger tomorrow. I can't wait to spend the rest of my life with you."

Brook snuggled into his arms and chuckled. "There's no rush on the ring, but that's good to know. Lots to look forward to."

Brad laughed along as he nudged her out of the booth. "My proposal will have to wait. Your fans are arriving."

Brook grinned as the bell over the bakery rang. She loved hearing that sound. She'd missed it so much in the church kitchen. But today's bell didn't signal just one or two people. To her surprise, more than a dozen people were walking in. A line began to form outside the door.

It was a good thing she'd asked Avery to bake extra cupcakes. She even had little finger sandwiches to sell. Seaside Cupcakes hadn't changed its name yet, but soon they'd be serving soup and sandwiches for lunch every day.

The booths and tables in the bakery filled with people eager to welcome Brook back to the neighborhood. Brook stayed behind the cash register, greeting and ringing up countless customers while Avery boxed up treats. She watched in shock as the line outside her bakery never quite ended.

Rachel waited patiently in line. When it was her turn to order, she rushed behind the counter to give her friends a hug. "I can't believe you're open again. With lunch choices! I'll be here for my lunch break. I'm so proud of you."

Brook squeezed her friend back, feeling tears form in her eyes. "I couldn't have done it without everyone's help. Thank you for supporting me."

Rachel smiled as she grabbed her cookies and swiped a credit card through the machine. "Well, I hope you like being busy. I have a feeling the town's going to support you for a very long time."

The shrill sound of an incoming message cut through the noisy crowd. Rachel pulled her phone out, her mouth popping into an O in surprise. "It's the doctor from the emergency room. He texted me. He wants to meet for lunch."

Brook threw her head back and laughed. "I told you he didn't want your phone number for the hospital fundraiser. Go ahead. Go on the date. You deserve to have a little fun with a cute doctor."

Rachel frowned at her friend. "You think he likes me? I'm sure he wants to talk about the hospital. He said something about getting the school involved. I guess he wants to have children there, since it's a children's hospital. And he knows I'm a teacher, so…"

Brook shook her head in amazement as her friend muttered to herself and walked out the door. Rachel could be so naive.

After more than an hour of working with customers, Avery bumped Brook from the cash register. "Take a break," she urged. "Brad's waiting for you in the kitchen. I can handle the crowds."

Brook didn't argue. It was amazing to see so many people out to support her, but she was a little tired from socializing. She shouldered her way through the kitchen door and into the quiet kitchen.

Brad had dragged two chairs together and set his crutches aside. As she walked into the room, he pulled a bouquet from behind his back and patted the empty seat next to him.

"It's not an engagement ring, but these flowers should brighten up the space." He gave her a wide grin, beaming with pride. "Congratulations, Brook. I hope your bakery is a success for a long, long time. I want to be here for every day of your happiness."

Brook leaned in for a long kiss, then took the flowers from him and settled into the empty chair. "That sounds like a great plan. Let's start forever together, right now."

Free Short Story

Avery and Grant's engagement story is now available, and it's exclusive to newsletter subscribers!

Sign up for Tori Mitchell's monthly newsletter at subscribepage.io/ToriMitchell to get a free copy of *Forever Home in Sunset Cove*. You'll be the first to know about upcoming books, discounts, and more.

Join the Kindness Committee!

THANK YOU FOR READING *Second Chances in Sunset Cove.* If you enjoyed Brook and Brad's story, please consider leaving a review on Amazon or Goodreads. Even a short review can help us reach new readers and spread more kindness.

How does a story spread kindness? **If you purchased this book, you've officially joined the Sunset Cove Kindness Committee!** Ten percent of profits from the Sunset Cove series are donated to non-profit organizations like the Child Life program at Children's Hospital of Philadelphia, which helps children facing a serious illness or hospitalization.

About the Author

TORI MITCHELL WRITES SWEET, small-town romance with a guaranteed Happily Ever After.

She found her own small-town happy ending in the Pocono Mountains of Pennsylvania, where she lives with her husband and two children. When she's not reading, writing or daydreaming about the beach, you'll find Tori growing an absurd amount of tomatoes and rhubarb in her garden.

Get the latest news on sales, new books, and more with Tori's newsletter at subscribepage.io/ToriMitchellnewsletter.

· ♥ · ♥ · ♥ · ♥ · ♥ ·

Printed in Great Britain
by Amazon